Smugglers of Sandhill Island

by

Peggy Chambers

Sandhill Island Series

Cover Art by *Tina Lynn Stout*

The Wild Rose Press, Inc.
PO Box 708
Adams Basin, NY 14410-0708
Visit us at www.thewildrosepress.com

Publishing History
First Edition, 2025
Trade Paperback ISBN 978-1-5092-6178-9
Digital ISBN 978-1-5092-6179-6

Sandhill Island Series
Published in the United States of America

Dedication

I would like to dedicate this novel to the readers who stuck with me throughout the Sandhill Island saga. The island will remain forever in my heart.

Chapter 1

Cody Brown stood barefoot in the tide pool watching the inhabitants. Blue-green waves tumbled over each other in unison foaming up on sugar white sand, leaving tiny crabs and fish behind. The next high tide would carry them back out to deeper water. In their tiny world, life would go on as it should until the giant ocean reclaimed it. When he was a child, he spent countless hours wading in tidepools and playing in the ocean with his sister, Dani. They didn't play anymore; in fact, they hardly spoke.

These days, Cody owed his drug dealer, Joey, a lot of money. He wasn't even sure how much with interest and everything. Math was not his thing. But he did know how desperate the situation was.

Cody never had the urge to make an honest living and work hard like his mother, or his sister. That was too much trouble. There were other ways to get money than the daily grind of nine to five. That was for schmucks. And he was no schmuck. But he needed to make a living like everyone else.

His sister had a business of her own and he was jealous. He always felt she was the favorite in the family. Maybe she was just a hard worker, but he didn't like that she always did better than him. He always told her she was the favorite because she was a girl, Mom liked her best, and so did their uncle Ralph. Anything to get under her skin.

"You sound like a snot-nosed kid when you say such things," Uncle Ralph said. "And you should keep that to yourself. You should work as hard as your sister and then you might amount to something."

That made things worse. And now and then in an argument, the favoritism would come up.

Cody was the youngest child by two years—the baby of the family. He could normally get out of trouble with his mother when he was a kid. Just one look peeking out from under his tousled brown hair with his blue eyes and she melted. Almost every time.

He was attractive to girls as he got older, too. Most of the time the eyes worked on them just like his mother. Most of the time. His sister called them puppy eyes. He had puppy eyes, and he knew how to use them to his best advantage. They even worked on Dani until he got older and she learned he was always up to something. Anything except work—which was a four-letter word.

Their father left when Cody was a baby. Mom always said it had nothing to do with them. The problem was her. He wondered. But Mom did her best to raise the two kids and her brother, Uncle Ralph, became like another parent. He was around a lot and he had a great houseboat. It was old but cool. They often spent weekends as a family there when his mom didn't have to work. Summers were the best; no school and the ocean was their playground.

Then Uncle Ralph left the houseboat to Dani when he died. It all had to do with the fact that Cody couldn't hold a job. It wasn't his fault; he wasn't cut out to be a fast-food worker and as far as fishing went, that was a lot of work.

Even though he was the younger sibling, he was male and he should have inherited his uncle's boat, right? Isn't that how things worked? But no, his sister got the houseboat. His sister lived there for free. He had to scrounge and sleep on friends' couches until they tired of him and threw him out.

He was right. She *was* the favorite. And it was also true he didn't really want to work as hard as Dani.

But this time he was in big trouble. He ran drugs for a dealer who now wanted his money back. Cody was unsure what had happened to all of the dealer's money. He was handed drugs to sell and bring the money back to his dealer. He had. He had also consumed some of the product himself—and maybe shared some with friends—so sometimes he was short when he took the proceeds back to his boss. Maybe that was it, but it wasn't like he stole the money. Maybe that was what Joey was miffed about. Somehow though, the money he owed had grown. The dealer told him the excessive debt had to do with the magic of compound interest. Whatever that meant. Joey said he accumulated interest on the unpaid balance. But whatever the problem, it was time to pay up and Cody didn't have the money.

Drug dealers knew exactly what they were doing when they turned a normal person into an addict. When the addict was desperate enough to do anything for a fix, the dealer could be relied on to give them a job. They gave them product to sell to someone else, and when they made a profit, the dealer would pay them with a fix for their addiction. It was the simplest form of economics, supply and demand. Not only did it show a profit; it created a new demand. As business went, it was brilliant. As humanity went, it was the devil's work.

Cody couldn't keep his hand out of the cookie jar. He knew he needed a different job—maybe something legal. But that probably would not happen in his lifetime. He was an addict with an expensive habit. And now he needed money, and he only had one place to get it—from his sister, Dani. He was her little brother and maybe she still loved him like she did when he was young. He wasn't sure. But he knew she would never run drugs for the dealers—she'd die before she'd let them force her into that. But the dealers were about to ask for her help and if she didn't give it, they would just take it.

Most days Cody felt the whole world was against him; first his family—what was left of them—and now Joey and his drug dealing bosses. But no matter who was against him or for him, it was possible he might not get out of this one alive.

Chapter 2

Dannielle Brown—Dani—made the daily trek from her houseboat, tied up in Corpus Christi where she lived, to her tour boat, *Wanderlust*—moored on Sandhill Island where she worked—then back home. Almost constantly on the water, she had trouble adjusting to solid ground. She had sea legs.

She felt safe on her ancient houseboat as the wind rocked the vessel, waves lapping at the hull of her home. It needed a paint job, but so far that was not on the agenda. Paint cost money—something that was in short supply.

Her uncle left her the houseboat when he died. She was always special to Uncle Ralph—a fact not lost on her baby brother, Cody. Uncle Ralph knew she loved the water, and he wanted her to be able to live and work where she was happiest.

Cody was a drifter with little ambition beyond where to get his next fix. Their uncle tried to get Cody interested in making a living off the ocean by becoming a fisherman or something. But Cody wasn't interested. Before Uncle Ralph died he said he hoped Cody would find his way someday. So far he hadn't.

The empty beer bottle almost slipped from her hand onto the deck as she nodded off. Time for bed. It was Dani's habit, when the weather was good, to sit on the deck of the houseboat and relax after dinner and a shower. Tomorrow was another workday and she'd have to hustle to make the first ferry to Sandhill Island and then walk to *Wanderlust* to pick up customers. The early bird always caught the worm, and she would be there early to catch as many tourists as her boat could cart around the tiny island.

Stretching her long, tanned, arms as she yawned, she carried the empty beer bottle to the trash container on the deck, then opened the door and stepped inside. Her shoulder-length brown hair still felt damp from the shower as she ran her fingers through it. Tomorrow it would be pulled back up in a ponytail with a faded baseball cap over it. Shorts, tee shirt, deck shoes, and a cap were her uniform most days.

Walking through the kitchen she twisted the lid to the cookie jar that sat on the counter. It was plastic and ugly. A teddy bear that had blue eyes she thought were frightening when she was young. It was something her mother had when she was a kid and it had a screw-on lid which made it a little more secure for some things. Inside was her life savings. Not much, but she put most of the money she made each day into it. She had to make monthly payments to the bank on *Wanderlust*. At least for now. She was almost finished paying for the boat and then her profit margin would improve. In the bedroom at the back of the boat, she pulled her nighttime shorts and tee shirt from the drawer and tossed them on the unmade bed. She had no idea why people made beds each day. They would only get messed up again at night.

She brushed her teeth as she looked at bloodshot eyes from days on the water squinting in the sun, and tan lines left by the sunglasses, and shook her head. Her youth was not as evident as it used to be.

She fell into bed in a heap, sheets and blankets shoved to the end, not covering her. The summer evenings were hot and humid, so all the windows were open. She switched on the oscillating fan that sat on the nightstand and sighed as it blew up and down her body in a rhythmic motion. She fell asleep almost immediately to the hum of the fan's motor.

The screens on the windows of the ancient houseboat often collected moisture from the sea air and then released it in a quick breeze, smacking Dani in the face with salt water. Normally, the light salt spray didn't wake her. But this time she snapped awake—she heard footsteps on the deck.

The front door rattled slightly, and then a quick click.

Dani silently opened the drawer of the bedside table and pulled out the .357 she kept loaded and near-at-hand. It was an extravagant expense she paid for once hoping to never have to use. When you were female and single it never hurt to be prepared. The dock where she kept her houseboat was normally safe, but you just never knew.

Swinging her feet over the edge of the bed and onto the floor, she stood with the revolver in front of her and moved toward the door. She was wide awake now. When the door opened, she saw a shaggy head poke in, then stumble into her living room.

"I don't know who you are but get out of my house now!" Dani dashed to the other end of the boat, the gun in front of her. But the intruder didn't seem to hear. Stumbling to the sofa, he collapsed face down on the cushions and promptly began to snore like the little brother she grew up with before Dad left, and Mom died.

"Cody! You asshole, what are you doing?" She

kicked his foot that hung off the edge and he jumped, turned his head, and looked at her with glazed eyes.

"Hi, Sis. I thought I'd pay you a visit," he lisped. Cody's eyes closed before the sentence left his mouth.

Cody Brown was stoned again. She had told him not to come here to sleep it off. For all the good her speech had done. He was back and passed out on her couch—again.

That's when she realized she stood over him with the gun still in her hand.

"Idiot," she breathed. "I could have blown you away. How would I explain that to Mom?" She often talked to Mom, knowing she was not there, but it gave her comfort, and she felt the woman still heard her though she could not talk back. Mom would not have been happy about this occurrence.

Cody snorted and drew his legs up in a fetal position looking like the little brother she once loved, then snored again his mouth hanging open.

There was no way he'd wake up now. Who knew where he'd been when he decided to stumble into his sister's place, jimmying the lock the way Uncle Ralph showed them. But it was obvious what he had been doing. She should be happy knowing he was safe here and not sleeping it off in a back alley. But she was tired of it. Mostly she was just tired, and she had to go to work in the morning. She'd deal with him then. She couldn't physically throw him out anyway. She turned and walked back to the unmade bed with the fan that blew across it. Exhaustion overtook her and she fell asleep almost immediately.

Just as the sky was beginning to pink, she was startled awake by snoring in her house. Falling back on the pillow, she remembered Cody. He was surely still on her aging green plaid sofa—the one left in the houseboat when Uncle Ralph died. It was old then and needed to be replaced, but she seldom sat on it.

Pouring juice into a clean glass as she waited on the toast to pop up, Dani looked at her brother still sleeping in the rising sun. She wanted to run him out before she left, knowing he could just get back in with the rigged lock on her home. She needed to have it replaced. But if she did, he might tear something up breaking in. The lock mirrored the age of the houseboat they had played on as kids.

Toast in hand, she walked to the sofa and once again kicked Cody's foot that hung off the edge. "Wake up, Cody."

He didn't even stir.

"Cody!" louder this time. "You need to leave. I have to go to work. Some of us work for a living, you know."

He rolled over onto his back, his long legs stretching off the end of the couch and opened one blue eye. "Hey, Dani. Thanks for letting me crash at your place last night. What time is it?" He looked around the room as if he'd find a clock. Uncle Ralph didn't use clocks. He worked from daylight until dark and passed that habit down to his niece.

"The sun says it is almost six and you have to go." She swallowed the toast and washed it down with juice.

Cody stretched long and loud. "You're going to leave your little brother with no breakfast?" He smiled his crooked smile. The one that he used on his girlfriends. The one that used to work on their mother, and even her, when she was younger.

"I made coffee, and you can take it with you in a to-go cup." She nodded to the cup that sat ready on the countertop by the door.

He eyed her toast, reaching out an unwashed hand. Hesitantly, she held it out in a gesture of friendship, though she didn't know why.

He shoved the half piece of toast in his mouth all at once and smiled as he chewed. Dani wondered when the last time was that he ate. "Um, blackberry. From Meg's garden?"

She nodded.

"Got any more?"

"No, Cody. You need to leave. I have to go to work."

He groaned. Slowly sliding one foot onto the floor he sat up and rubbed a hand across his face, shook his shaggy brown hair once more back into his eyes, and stood. "Okay, I'm leavin'. Nice way to treat your only brother, throwin' him out with no breakfast. Mom said we had to stick together."

"But Mom's not here. Don't forget your coffee." Dani reached for the to-go cup sitting on the counter and held it out to her brother, but he waved her away and stumbled out the door. If he left without even coffee, she looked that much worse. She knew how he played people; he always had, even when he was little.

The door slammed shut behind him.

Chapter 3

Joseph Rossi was just Joey to anyone who knew him. Using a last name in his business was asking for trouble. He knew he needed a haircut and was unsure when he took his last shower, but hygiene wasn't that important to him. He stepped out into the hot Corpus Christi summer sun then walked to his once black sedan which was as grimy as the windows he tried to look through while driving. It no longer had a color, just a dusty gray. Opening the car door, he found clutter and used cups from trips involving drive-through restaurants. He needed to wash her. Or maybe he'd have someone do it for him. Manual labor, especially in the heat, was not in his nature. He hated hands-on work which was why nothing ever got done. He could find plenty of flunkies to do it for him. First, he'd need to make sure there was nothing of value in it for them to take to the local pawn shop.

From behind the steering wheel, he gazed through the smeared window. He wanted to upgrade his ride. He had his eye on a black onyx Cadillac Escalade and knew a guy who could get him a good deal. And he'd keep it clean this time; you could bet on that. But he'd never park it in this neighborhood. Parking an Escalade around here was a sure way to wake up finding it gone or stripped. Sometime soon, when he could get someone to take his place and he could move up in the company.

Corpus was full of high-rise apartments with garages underneath to keep his new ride secure. But before anything else, he had to make sure the new man could be trusted. He couldn't leave the clientele behind when he moved on. Someone had to take care of them and keep the money coming in. They were out here every day waiting on him. They were his bread and butter.

He wiped away some grime on the windshield and saw that they were once more waiting on him. The vultures were sitting on the curb looking his way. They knew he had the stuff if they had the money. They were vultures, but they were his bread and butter. Without them he wouldn't have a business. The ones who could be trusted weren't around this morning. Cody had been one of those—at one time. He could send Cody on an errand, and he returned with the job done. In fact, he had Cody in mind to take his place someday. Lately, though, Cody had been putting too much of the product up his nose. That often happened to the good ones. They liked the product too much. Now, Cody owed him money and the time had come to pay up. Cody said he had something happening on Mustang Island that would be a good money maker. Joey hoped so, for his sake, because Cody's time was up.

Joey was giving Cody one more chance before he pulled in his sister. He'd heard Cody's sister had a tour boat and that was just what he needed. A tour boat could make the rounds from Corpus to Sandhill and other islands where the summer tourists stayed, without attracting attention. In fact, even if Cody did pay up, Joey might still try to pull the sister in. She could be very helpful.

He could take his product to Sandhill Island where

the tour boat docked, then Cody's sister could meet the cigar boats in the open water. The cigar boats could outrun most any Coast Guard vessel on the water if the driver knew what he was doing. They often made deliveries to offshore oil rigs and other boats beyond prying eyes on the shore.

Joey would ask around to find out where Cody's sister, Dani, tied up her houseboat. He'd heard she lived on one boat and made her living on another. Boats! Some people and their boats. Frankly, he'd keep his feet on solid ground and get others to do the work out on the water for him. Yes, Cody could be of some help. But he needed persuasion. And if Cody didn't come through with the money, Dani might find her happy home at the bottom of the ocean. That could be very persuasive.

Joey leaned over and opened the glovebox stuffed full of trash and raked it into the floorboard for the flunky to clean up later. Reaching deep inside, he retrieved the revolver. Stuffing it in his belt under the dirty tee shirt, he sat back up and looked again at the losers sitting on the curb. He pulled the knife he always had with him from his pocket and began to clean the grime from under his fingernails while he considered who to send on the errand. Later, he would probably cut an apple with the same blade that had never seen soap and water.

"Ernie!" he shouted at the biggest loser of the bunch. This guy would take anything to get high. The dirty homeless man looked up and smiled a toothless smile, then stumbled his way.

Joey stepped out of the car and dangled the keys in front of the man's face. "Clean this up for me will you? There'll be something good in it for you when you're done."

Ernie smiled showing rotten teeth and took the keys. "And be careful with her. She's a classic."

Joey walked back inside the apartment that mirrored his transportation and stepped into the bedroom. Beside the unmade bed, deep in the closet that was crammed with junk, he had a safe and it was full of what the customers outside were waiting for.

He turned the dial and opened the metal door taking out just enough to sell to the addicts that waited outside. Give them just enough to keep them alive and coming back.

He stepped from the apartment and crossed to where the men sat on the curb.

"Good morning, gentlemen," he said and smiled.

They crowded around.

As Joey was finishing the morning sales, Cody got in line.

"Morning, boss," Cody said with a crooked smile.

"We need to talk," Joey said and jerked his head toward the apartment. This needed to be done in private.

Chapter 4

As soon as Joey collected the money from the morning run, he shoved Cody up the stairs and inside the door. He didn't say anything in front of all the prying eyes out in the parking lot. Then he closed the door behind them.

"Relax, Joey; I'll get the money for you. Haven't I always?" Cody tried to smile.

Cody thought he could actually see steam come from the drug dealer's ears. That wasn't possible, he knew, but the man's brown eyes narrowed into black slits.

"Time's up, Cody," he said reaching for the addict's neck.

Quicker than Cody could imagine, he found himself pressed against the closed door of the grimy apartment. Joey's forearm was against his windpipe, and he gasped for air. Cody was nose to nose with the man he owed money and smelled his stagnant breath.

Trembling, Cody said, "Just give me a little more time. I've always worked hard for you, Joey."

Joey breathed hot breath in Cody's face. "Like I said, time's up." He pressed a little harder. "You were supposed to have it yesterday—and still you don't. But I have a new idea for how you can pay me back. You have a sweet sister. Dani, you call her? Dani has money. We'll talk to Dani."

"She lives day to day…money…based on customers." Cody tried not to gasp. Breathing was becoming harder and speaking almost impossible. He began to feel lightheaded, and he knew eventually the forearm would crush his windpipe and kill him.

Joey sighed. "But she has a boat, and I need product moved on a boat. She will work for me, and maybe she can pay off your debt. I'm tired of asking you to talk to her, Cody. I'm gonna talk to her myself. And I'm not going to ask nicely. She will move product for me. It won't be that big of a deal. She'll take the product out to the boats in the open water and her little brother will live. It's as simple as that. She's your sister. She does want you alive, right?" He pushed harder with his arm on Cody's neck.

Death was fast approaching from the nearly crushed windpipe. Cody knew he had to act. If Joey killed him, he'd still go after Dani. If he survived, maybe he could protect her somehow. He had to make Joey believe he could get Dani's help. Cody began to see stars but was determined not to pass out.

"Okay, okay. I'll make her…transport the stuff. She doesn't want me dead." Cody hoped Dani wouldn't let him die. Sadly, he wasn't sure anymore.

Joey eased up on the windpipe and Cody gasped. "I'll tell her tonight when she gets home."

"You'd better." Joey stepped back allowing Cody to breathe.

Cody grabbed his neck and gasped. Slowly his breathing came easier through the now swollen esophagus. His vision was returning and he needed to leave before Joey tried to kill him once more. He was used to living by his wits on the streets, but now he had to keep himself and Dani alive. Even though there were problems between them, he still loved his sister.

Cody rubbed his neck and nodded then opened the door and left before Joey changed his mind.

Chapter 5

Standing on the dock with a few other travelers, Dani waited on the ferry that crossed to Sandhill Island a few times a day. A to-go cup of coffee in one hand, she carried the small cooler that held her lunch in the other. A woman and tired looking child waited with her. The woman wiped her lined face of sweat from the early morning sun and the boy hid behind his mother smiling shyly. Dani lowered her sunglasses to wink at him. He giggled shrinking back behind his mother.

The only other pedestrian on the ferry was a man of undetermined age. He wore baggy clothes and a large-brimmed fisherman's hat down low over dark sunglasses. He was short, stocky, and appeared to be alone. Maybe a fisherman? Or a tourist? Dani didn't ever remember seeing him on the island, so he was probably just a day tripper. Unless the people were touring with her on her boat, she normally didn't watch them.

Dani tried to catch the first ferry of the day so she could be at *Wanderlust* as early as possible. The first ferry left at seven a.m. and that meant she could be at the place where she docked by seven-thirty. Most vacationers didn't rise too early, but she wanted to be available to anyone interested in a tour of the harbor and island even if they came back later. Sales were important.

The dock where *Wanderlust* was moored housed

many vessels these days. It had been rebuilt after a hurricane a few years back and now even Winter Texans tied up and lived there. Dani had a slip rented for her tour boat and the dock was well maintained with security twenty-four hours a day and well-lit at night.

Wanderlust, her little tour boat announced in peeling red paint trimmed in gold. She liked the font of the advertisement—an old English script. Someday, she'd like to paint the boat to look like an old British schooner. Maybe in black and gold like a pirate ship. It would attract attention. She might even install a mast with fake sails unfurled. Someday.

The boat had to be repainted soon. The salty wind could peel paint in a season; and unlike her houseboat, the tour boat had to be pristine. Travelers needed to believe they were going out on a sea-worthy vessel and not end up like Gilligan's passengers on a three-hour tour. The fresher the paint, the more successful, and safe, the tour boat appeared. She'd talk to Shayla about repainting the lettering and worry about the rest of it later.

She bought the used touring boat a few years ago from a guy in Rockport and made monthly payments to the bank on the jet-driven boat. It had no propellers making it dolphin, and other sea life, safe. Powered by a 300 H.P. John Deere Marine Diesel engine, it was powerful enough to take the waves if they got stuck out in bad weather. She tried not to let that happen when the thirty-four-foot-long, U.S. Coast Guard certified vessel was full and carrying thirty-six passengers. Or even if it only carried two. Most tourists didn't like storms on the ocean. Dani wasn't crazy about them either.

Her uncle thought it was bad luck to name a boat.

The houseboat wasn't named, but eventually Dani felt the need to name the touring boat, *Wanderlust,* because she could never stay in one place—at least on land. So, she wandered the ocean.

She ran a hand over the rough texture of her boat. It sat bobbing up and down in the sparkling water, when she heard a series of clicks and whistles from the air sacs located behind the blowhole belonging to Scar—her favorite dolphin. Not that she knew a lot of dolphins personally, just the one, but he was still her favorite. She'd named him that because of the scar that streaked across his head, probably from a boat propeller. It wasn't deep or jagged, so it probably did little damage when he was injured. But it was her way of recognizing the mammal when he greeted her each morning. The ocean was full of dolphins, but his presence always made her happy.

"Hey, Scar!" He smiled back at her. Dolphins always smiled, it seemed to Dani, and maybe that was why she liked him so much. But like a good dog, Scar was faithfully at her side most days as she started the tour boat. Once out of the harbor, he'd sometimes entertain her guests by flying out of the water and landing on his belly—drenching the sweltering humans on board.

Stepping to the controls, Dani started the engine. It was a normal thing each morning just to hear the engine purr. She'd pull to the other side of the dock and fuel the thirsty tank. She filled the tank daily and it became her largest monthly expense except for the payment to the bank. At ten dollars a head, slightly lower than her competitors, she could make $360 an hour if the boat were full. Each tour was an hour long, but she normally ran only two each morning and two each afternoon.

Evening tours happened seldom—only if the customers had something special in their lives. Most tourists were done with daily activities by supper time. If she had a full boat four times a day, she could make over $1400 a day. On a good day. With a full boat.

That never happened.

But she could make over $10,000 a week, if the boat ran without repairs, she never needed fuel, the weather held up, the tourists weren't cheap, and they filled her little vessel to capacity.

They didn't.

But sometimes the tourists tipped. She considered that gravy and stuck the money in her pocket. It was a small pocket and never got over-full.

At the end of the dock where she filled the ever-hungry fuel tank of her boat was a bait shop. She'd buy a fish just for Scar from the change in her pocket. She liked keeping him around for the tourists as well as herself. He was good company.

Looking across the dock she saw a crowd of three or four people standing near where she tied up her tour boat. Maybe if she had a bucket of fish, Scar would entertain and keep the customers happy.

"Gimmie a small bucket of the bait shad," she told Jimmy, the worker, as she paid for the fuel.

****

Jimmy Carpenter had worked for the Stanford Trust all his young life. His father helped him get the job fueling boats on the dock after school. Really, Dad had talked to Meg and just announced at dinner one night Jimmy was to report to the dock after school the next day. It was shortly after the debacle with the firecrackers in the lunchroom.

His father stood from his chair that night when Jimmy started to complain about what his mother had fixed for dinner. "You're lucky to have something for dinner. Your mother works hard for us. And I don't take kindly to my only son not being a good student who doesn't follow the rules. You weren't raised that way. So, I'll keep you busy so you won't have time to run around with hoodlums who would ruin your life."

Jimmy knew that look on his father's face. He'd seen it before, and he meant business. It was just a goof, the incident with the firecrackers, but it wouldn't happen again. Dad would see to that.

So, no questions asked, Jimmy reported to the fishy smelling dock after school the next day and every day thereafter. When he graduated high school he just never left. His intention was to leave Sandhill Island as soon as school was out and head for Corpus Christi. He would get off this stinkin' island and live in the big city. He and Smitty had a plan. They'd get jobs in the city and room together. They knew there was more to life than the little island where they grew up.

Then Smitty's dad took him to the recruiting office to join the army. His son would serve as he had, and they could talk about college after he got out.

Smitty did as he was told.

It was shortly thereafter that Jimmy started dating Marybeth. The dream was gone, but Jimmy still planned to save his money and move to the mainland as soon as possible. Dating was new to him and soon all the money he had saved for the move slipped through his hands.

Marybeth lived with her mother and helped out with her care. Mom was sick a lot, or maybe Mom was just lazy, but Marybeth took care of her. She got a job at a taco stand on the beach and was home to help her mother every night.

"Every night? She can't even fix her own meal?" he asked when she said she had to get home to her mother.

"No, Jimmy, or bathe herself. I have to go. But I'll see you tomorrow night."

Jimmy thought that was a crock. But Marybeth went home to her mom every night after she and Jimmy met for a while after her shift.

It wasn't long before Marybeth announced to him that she thought she was pregnant.

"Pregnant? I kinda just thought that you were taking care of the birth control. I guess I never really asked—just assumed."

"Oh, Jimmy. The man is supposed to have the condoms."

And he knew he was hooked. Now he'd never leave the island because of Marybeth and the kid. She wouldn't leave her mother and he had responsibilities to the girl he got pregnant. He had no idea how he was going to tell his dad. But he knew he'd run if he had the money. He'd miss Marybeth but it was better than facing his dad or becoming a dad himself.

A few days later he met Joey on the dock. He was a greasy-looking character who appeared now and then and wanted to look over the dock.

"Just look the other way. There's money in it for you." Joey offered money to Jimmy to not tell anyone about him. Jimmy needed the money and so what? Joey didn't seem to be doing anything wrong, just looking around. What did it matter if Jimmy didn't tell anyone about him. Who would he tell anyway?

So, he took the money.

Then the guy with the broom and the hat started hanging around too and Jimmy began to wonder what was happening on the tiny island. There was never any excitement around here, so why now?

But he liked it.

He liked watching the comings and goings of the new people on the island. Maybe there was some stimulation on Sandhill Island after all. And who knew, if he did a good job for Joey, maybe he'd have a job for him in Corpus. He knew that the man came over on the ferry when he visited, so he just assumed he was from Corpus. He hadn't asked.

The guy in the hat was anyone's guess.

But for now, he'd fuel the vessels of his neighbors while he watched and learned. This wasn't like sitting in a classroom; this was real life.

Chapter 6

As Dani skimmed along the water to her slip, the people who waited walked away to the larger boats down the way. She wasn't fast enough. And another group of tourists were lost to the big guys. She sighed and then pulled into her slot once more and waited for the next round of customers.

Up by the office, she saw the man she'd seen earlier on the ferry. Short and stocky, he wore dark baggy clothes, and a large-brimmed green fishing hat pulled down over his sunglasses. He shuffled when he walked and carried a broom. He swept the area as he strolled down the sidewalk, then emptied the long-handled dustpan into trash cans along the way. Dani wasn't involved in the City of Sandhill Island business, but she didn't think anyone had been hired to keep the sidewalks clean. But it looked like a good idea. Tourists could be such slobs.

Tying up, she climbed out of *Wanderlust* and walked down the dock. Poppy and his dog were sitting in their normal fishing place. She patted his dog, Blackie, on the head and spoke to Poppy, a long-time resident of the island who knew everyone.

"Poppy, do you know who that is sweeping the sidewalk?" she asked.

"The Cleaner? I call him The Cleaner cause he told me that's what he does. I don't know his name. Oh, you have a customer," Poppy said, nodding toward her boat. "I think he got in all by himself. He shouldn't do that, should he? I started to tell him he needed to wait, then I saw you coming."

Dani glanced down the dock and could see someone lolling on the bench seat with a hat down over his eyes. Who would just help themselves to a boat they didn't own?

"Thanks, Poppy," she said and trotted toward her boat. The closer she got, the shaggy hair sticking out from under the hat seemed more familiar. Cody. Even though he helped himself to her boat, she hoped he was okay. She was about to find out. But she knew he would want a favor.

"Cody," she said walking up to her boat and opening the gate to step in. "Just help yourself, why don't you."

He raised his head, smiled, and pulled down the sunglasses on his face. "Hi, sis. Nice day, huh?"

"Well, it's better in the shade and at least a breeze has come up. It's going to be a hot one. What's up with you? What do you need? I know it's something, or you wouldn't be here. And is that a bruise on your neck?"

He absentmindedly pulled his collar closed. "Now, sis, what makes you think I need something other than to see my big sister?"

"History. I know you, Cody. You come around when you want something. What is it today?"

"A ride. Well, a friend of mine and I need a ride out to meet another boat. It won't take long, and he pays well."

Dani looked at her brother sitting in the shade on her hard-earned boat and knew something was wrong. "He pays well for a ride, huh. And why me? Why couldn't he get that boat to just come in and pick him up?"

Cody shoved the sunglasses back over his eyes and looked out to sea. A sure sign he was about to make up a lie. "The other boat can't come in this far. We just have to get out into open water. Three miles. It won't take an hour and he'll pay for the gas and your time. I don't see that you have a lot of customers today. I just climbed on your boat without anyone else around. We'd be doing you a favor."

She shook her head. She knew he was up to no good, as usual. "No. I don't know your friend or what you're up to. You need to go." Absentmindedly she tossed a fish to Scar who jumped in the air to catch it.

Cody sat up on the edge of the bench and took off his hat, wiping his face with his hand. "Sis, I'm in trouble and I need this. I wouldn't ask if it wasn't important."

"No! You always need something. Why can't you get a job like the rest of us and learn to take care of yourself?"

"It's just this once, sis. Look, he'll pay you."

"What have you gotten yourself into, Cody? Who wants the use of my boat that badly and why?"

Cody reached in the bucket and picked up a shad that lay shining in the sun. He tossed it to the dolphin who hung around his sister's boat. Of course, Scar caught it. "Just out about three miles and meet another boat. You drop us off, we pay you, you take your boat back to the harbor. That is all you have to do and I'm off the hook."

"Three miles, huh? Out into the open ocean—away from prying eyes."

"Dani, I'm in trouble. I owe some bad guys some real money, and this is the only way I can get them off my back. They already knew about you and your boat. They brought it up. I didn't mention you to them. I just need you to take me out to meet the boat, and then I'll be square with them. If you don't—bad stuff is going to happen." He reached in the bucket once more tossing the fish to the smiling mammal.

"Did they do that to you?" Dan nodded at Cody's bruised neck.

He shrugged.

"You have to go. You're scaring off my customers." She watched as another potential customer walked away toward the larger boats at the end of the dock. So far there were no customers today.

Dani doubted Cody was in real trouble, until she saw his bruised neck. He probably just wanted money, and she didn't have the kind of money he would want. Being semi-homeless, he drifted from friend to friend, and couch to couch, until they tired of him and threw him out. She was probably his last resort. There had been enough arguments between them in the past that he knew her opinion of his lifestyle. He knew—he just didn't care. She'd move heaven and earth to get him into rehab, but he wouldn't stay. Or the lessons learned there wouldn't stick.

They took turns tossing the shad to Scar. It seemed the only thing they had in common these days. They grew up together. Dani wondered how they could have grown so far apart? "Cody, I don't have any money to loan you. What happened to your neck?"

"I don't know. I woke up bruised this morning," he said and leaned in to talk. "Okay, if you won't take my friend, I need a ride to Mustang Island instead. Just you and me. It's been ages since we took a trip together. We could ride down there together and pitch a tent on the beach. A little vacation."

"Mustang Island is thirty miles away. While we're lolling on the beach, I'm missing out on some fares. I can't afford to take a vacation. Maybe someday, but not now in the height of the tourist season."

Cody ran his hands through his hair and looked up. "Sis, I really need this. I need the money and if you won't help my friend, there is a deal on Mustang where I can make some money. I don't have any other way to get there. I don't have a car. And I'm your baby brother," he said smiling.

"I know you're my brother, and I know you're up to something shady. I can't help you." Dani looked down the dock and saw people heading her way. She stood and waved.

"It's important. I have a business deal that will get me a lot of money. And I need it now."

Dani looked back at her brother. "Cody, I'm not going to be involved in a drug deal. And I also have business deals to attend to."

"It's not a drug deal,. I promise."

"No."

They reached in the fish bucket at the same time and looked up. He reached for her hand.

"I said no, Cody. I know you and your deals."

"Sis, it's important. I need some money. I…um…I owe some guys some money and they don't take no for an answer. I'm late on a payment. This is the only way I can make the money in time."

"Maybe if you'd get a real job, you wouldn't have these problems. I was just thinking about getting another boat. If I did, I'd need another tour captain. Maybe you could go to work for me."

He stood and looked out into the water. "Go to work for my big sister, huh? Yeah, that'll be the day. I just need this one thing. If I can get this done, my problems will be over."

"Your problems won't be over until you learn to leave the stuff alone, Cody. Let me get you some help. I'll gladly go into debt to get you clean and sober. And eventually we could become partners."

"Yeah, on your schedule. If we did everything your way, you could see your way to helping your little brother." He glared at her with his icy blue eyes.

"Try it out. There's a family headed this way, and you can give them a tour of the island. You can keep the money you make. Take *Wanderlust* and give it a whirl."

Cody looked at her with distrust, then his eyes softened. "Okay, sis, just this once."

Dani stepped back onto the dock.

Chapter 7

A small girl wearing a pink life jacket and matching hat jumped clapping her hands as she ran toward the tour boat.

"Ahoy!" Cody called and waved a hand at the people waiting. "Good morning," he said smiling.

The little girl jumped even higher, her floppy hat bobbing in the breeze. "Boat! Boat!" she squealed each time her sandals hit the wood.

A young woman in a hat that matched the girl's stepped forward. "We just got to the island and wanted to take our daughter on a tour. They told us at the beach rental there are dolphins around here and Suzy just loves dolphins."

"We do have dolphins sometimes." Almost on cue, Scar splashed Cody as if to say, *where's the fish?* "In fact, here's one now. I call him Scar. See the scar on his head? I think he probably got hit with a propeller. Scar normally sticks pretty close to shore, and we've become friends. Here, I'll show you." He stepped to the bucket and pulled a fish out holding it by the tail. Its silver scales shimmered in the sun as he tossed it to the dolphin. Scar caught the fish easily and swallowed it whole. He whistled and squeaked to thank him then dove under splashing everyone in his wake.

Cody laughed. "Scar is a character. Anyone who thinks animals don't have a sense of humor—well they're just wrong." He looked down the dock for more customers and didn't see anyone coming. "I charge ten dollars for adults and five for children under five. I see she already has her life jacket. That's good. I have some on the boat if you don't have your own." The father reached in his billfold and pulled out the money handing it over, and Cody helped the family board. "Find a place to sit anywhere. I just ask that you not move around once the boat gets under way."

Cody retrieved life jackets for the parents and donned his own. He knew the routine even if he didn't do it every day like Dani. Uncle Ralph had taught him well. He checked and double checked his instruments once more. The fuel gauge read full, and he verified it again even though Dani had just filled it. It didn't look like anyone else was coming.

He'd confirmed the weather on his radio;,the winds were light creating gentle waves. The engine was running smoothly. He moved toward the steps that enabled people to climb in the boat and stored them aside and out of the way.

"Okay folks. It looks like it will just be us this morning…"

"Wait, wait!" a long-legged young woman ran her direction pulling her male companion behind her. They skidded to a stop giggling right in front of her boat with money in hand.

"Is it too late for a ride?" the young woman asked.

"No, of course not. It will be ten dollars a head," Cody said as the woman thrust a twenty-dollar bill in his hand. Cody moved the steps once more, allowing the young couple to board and then put them back out of the way.

"Have a seat anywhere but please don't move around after the boat starts to travel. Here are your life jackets."

"Is it okay to sit on them? I hate to wear a life jacket. Tan lines, you know," the woman said with a smile.

"That's fine. Adults don't have to wear them. I just want you to have them. The seas are calm, and the vessel is seaworthy. The precaution of life jackets is just that, a precaution." Cody could be a showman when he needed to be.

Cody unhooked his ropes and began to back the boat out of the cove where the dock was built. He waved at the other boats along the way and most people waved back. Sandhill Island was a community, and he knew most everyone unless they were summer tourists.

He began the speech into the mic that Dani delivered every time she took a group out and around the tiny island. He'd heard it many times. "Sandhill Island is a town of fishermen and business owners. The small island is approximately two miles wide and about four miles long. It is connected to the mainland by way of a ferry that runs four times a day. Unless you own your own boat, you travel by ferry into Corpus Christi."

He felt a tug on his shirt and turned around. The little girl in the pink hat was standing behind him.

"Where's your dolphin? I want to see your dolphin."

"Annie, remember you are to stay in your seat." Her mother pulled the child back to the bench on the side of the boat. "Sorry," she said and glanced up knowingly at Cody who smiled.

"No problem."

Splash! A wave of water came up over the bow of the boat and hit Cody right in the face. He took off his sunglasses and wiped the water from his eyes then held a hand up to cover the glare from the water. He slowed the boat to an idle.

"Annie, I think we found your dolphin."

Scar came up out of the water next to the boat, began his conversation with whistles and chirps, and quickly dove back under to race away from the boat.

"Oh!" Annie bounced on her toes. "I wanna to ride 'im!" She shouted and clapped her hands.

"I doubt he'll let you ride him. But maybe we can feed him some fish." Cody chuckled and picked up the bucket holding it out for the little girl who stepped back holding her nose. "They're a little stinky, but Scar loves them. He seems to have adopted this boat, and he follows me around sometimes. Here, I'll show you." He picked up the silver fish by the tail and held it over the side of the boat.

In a flash the dolphin once more appeared with his trademark smile and cackled at the boat of tourists. He was a ham, loving the attention—and the fish. The ocean was full of them, but he liked Cody and Dani's the best. Tossing the fish in the air, the dolphin catapulted after it, swallowing it whole, and then landed on his belly splashing the entire boat.

Annie giggled. Salt water dripped off the pink hat and into her eyes.

"You want to try?" Cody asked.

This time Annie dove into the bucket with both hands and threw two hands full of shad over the side of the boat. She wiped her hands down the side of her clothes. Her father instantly appeared beside her.

"Here, hon, let me show you. One at a time." He picked up a single fish and held it up for the dolphin to see then tossed it out into the water.

The boat suddenly dipped sideways as all the occupants stood on the side where the dolphin fed.

"Whoa, folks. We need to keep the vessel balanced. Let's feed our guest from both sides of the boat." Cody dumped the bucket of fish into a second container and handed it to the woman who was concerned about tan lines not ten minutes ago. With a smile as wide as Annie's, she then shoved her companion aside and held out a fish for the dolphin to snag.

It didn't take Scar long to realize he could get fed from both sides of the boat. He could easily glide under and scoop up breakfast from more than one hand. And he did, until the buckets were empty. He then disappeared.

"Okay, that's all for the dolphin. Scar is done once the fish are gone. But he'll be back. It's a great big ocean but he likes our little island."

As he cruised back, Cody pointed out signs to the passengers. "On the left is Le Chez, the best restaurant on the island at least according to Chef Sam. He is known for his dinner rolls as well as his fish entrees. And that huge garden behind the fancy house is where a lot of Chef Sam's food comes from. But most importantly we have a jazz singer from Corpus. Maybe you've heard of her. Billie Stone sings the blues and jazz on the weekends. She was born and raised here. We're very proud of her. The ferry to the mainland is coming up and we'll slow down to allow them to disembark..." He throttled back and waited on the ferry.

Cody droned on and on as he made the trip around the island. He pulled the tour boat expertly into the slip and helped his customers climb back onto the dock. He gathered the life jackets and placed the steps where his passengers could climb out.

"Thank you for riding with *Island Tours*. Come back to see Scar and me anytime. We're always here."

That was when he spied the man with the greasy black hair on the dock talking to the boy who ran the fueling station. Joey was on Sandhill Island. The smile disappeared from Cody's face, and he pulled his hat down over his eyes.

When the customers were gone, he turned and looked his sister in the eye. "I don't see me doing that day in and day out. It's fine for you, but not for me."

The old Cody was back. Dani sighed.

He glanced once more toward the fuel tanks. "Now will you take me to Mustang Island?" he asked.

"No, Cody. Find your own way to Mustang Island." She gestured for him to leave.

Cody sighed. "See ya, Scar." Shaking his head, he tossed the money on the captain's chair. Cody jumped onto the dock and stomped away without a word; his hands stuffed in his pockets.

Dani took off her sunglasses and rubbed her eyes. She felt like a low life. How could she treat her brother like that? She knew that was what he was thinking. He was accustomed to getting his own way. Her mother had given in to him all the time as they grew up and he knew just how to twist her to do his bidding. Dani couldn't, and wouldn't, do that. She wanted him to learn to rely on himself. But she knew what he was capable of doing. She might not know exactly, but she was aware that he would do something illegal to get the money he owed.

Maybe she should try harder with Cody. Maybe she should have helped him after all. She sighed. He always left her feeling guilty.

Chapter 8

Cody walked away from his sister's boat and headed for the ferry. Sticking his hand in his pocket he almost came up empty. He had just enough money to get back to Corpus Christi on the ferry. He probably should have kept the money from the tour, but he tossed it back at Dani to make her feel bad. He needed to find a ride to Mustang Island before Joey spied him. If he didn't get the money, he was going to die. He wasn't kidding when he told his sister that.

As he passed the ice cream shop, he saw the dark-haired woman in cut-off overalls squatted down next to the window. Shayla was the local artist and was hired by many of the businesses in town. She probably had a job repainting the shop's glass. If he had any artistic talent, maybe he could get a job painting designs for people. If he had any talent at all. He never had. The only thing he could do was bat his eyelashes and try to talk people into doing things for him. And sometimes it worked. In fact, most of the time it worked on almost everyone but his sister.

He hated to admit it, but Dani was probably right about he'd never amount to anything until he left the stuff alone. But he doubted that would happen. And right now, he had bigger problems to worry about. If he didn't get that money to Joey by the end of the week, his problems would be over because he would be dead. Joey had made that perfectly clear.

Maybe Shayla might give him a ride. Maybe he could talk her into an evening on the beach. He knew she had a car and an apartment somewhere around here.

"Hey, pretty lady." Cody walked up on the wooden sidewalk that ran the length of the shops in the downtown area of Sandhill Island. He had no idea why the island didn't pour concrete instead of constructing wooden planks that were always in need of repair. He knew the concrete would last longer, but maybe the old-style decking was quainter.

She turned and smiled. She was a classic Caribbean beauty. Her jet-black dreadlocks were wound into a braid at the back of her head and covered with a bandana to keep the paint off. He admired how she made a pair of ragged cut off overalls look that good, but her shiny dark skin glowed in the afternoon sun as she painted pictures of ice cream dripping from a cone.

"Hey, Cody. What's up?"

"Oh, you know, just visiting the island. I see you have a job. I wish I could paint. Maybe you could teach me some time."

Shayla wiped a spot of paint from her face. "You want to learn to paint, huh?" Her eyes narrowed.

"I don't know. Do you think I could learn?"

"My grandma told me you could do anything you set your mind to. And my mind went to art. Maybe yours works a little bit differently."

She stood and stepped back, eyeing her work. "There, I think that's what the owner wanted. She's not in today so I think I'll clean up and check with her tomorrow. Then maybe I'll get paid." She closed up the paint cans and wiped her brushes on the rag that hung from her back pocket.

"Here, let me help you," Cody smiled at her and picked up the drop cloth after she replaced the paint cans into her rolling tote. "So, what are your plans for the rest of the day?"

"I need to go visit my mother in Corpus. You?"

"I need to get to Mustang Island, and I thought my sister might take me, but she's busy. You know anyone going that way? I thought about hitching. I gotta see a guy." He didn't tell her he was picking up a package to be delivered to Corpus and it was probably drugs. She didn't ask.

"You have bus fare? I could get you to the station and you'd be on the island by 5:00."

"I'm a little low on funds right now." He looked down at his shoes trying to look pitiful.

"Well, maybe, if you shake out that drop cloth and help me get it to the car, I could front you the bus fare." She smiled, showing pearly teeth.

"You'd do that for me?" He glanced up shyly.

"Of course. You'd do it for me. What are friends for?"

He picked up the drop cloth, shaking it free of dried paint, then folded it placing it on the rolling tote. "Which way to your car?"

****

Cody raced down the jetty to where the boat should've been moored. The charter boat took tourists out to the red snapper banks to fish. The crew helped the tourists reel in their catch and sometimes even cut it up for them to take home and cook. There was a guy on the red snapper boat that had some product that he wanted Cody to transport for him. He had to be there on time. He had to. The guy didn't say how much money he'd make but at the moment, any amount was good.

The *Big Tuna* docked at the end of the pier, but he saw nothing there. And the farther he ran, still nothing. He'd missed the first ferry to Port Aransas, the only town on the island, because of bus schedules. He almost didn't get on the second one because of the crowd. The ferry could only hold so many. He was told the boat left at six o'clock and it was almost six twenty when he arrived. He knew the slip was at the end of the pier and his legs were pumping racing past fishermen and tourists. But when he reached the end of the wharf, it was only a dot.

Cody gasped for breath leaning over, hands on his knees. He was only in his mid-twenties—well all right late twenties. But he shouldn't be in this bad of shape. He had once been on the high school track team. Now his lungs screamed for oxygen from the short jaunt. Holding his hand up to shade his eyes, he looked out to sea. The dot was moving away. A coin-fed binocular grabbed his attention. Docks often had them so people could see boats, dolphins, sea birds, and the ocean up close and personal that were far away. He dug through his dirty cargo shorts for the last quarter he had to his name. His finger went through a hole in the bottom, and he came up empty of any change. Just his luck.

He moved away to the end of the dock and stared out into the evening ocean where the waves were laying down along with the breeze. It would turn into a beautiful evening that he might enjoy if he weren't so miserable. How had he gotten to this place in his life? No money, nowhere to live without crashing on someone's couch, and no prospects.

"Yeah, it's gonna' be a beautiful evening," said a

voice behind him.

An aging fisherman with tackle box and rod in hand leaned over and looked through the binoculars in the direction of the dot Cody had just seen. Cody felt a pang of jealousy as the man fed another coin into the machine.

"See anything?" Cody asked as the man once more bent to peer through the glass.

"Just a boat. Wish I was on it." The old man sighed. "You ever been out on the sea at night, just you and the stars? There's nothing like it in the world. I spent twenty years in the Navy, and I love a moonlit night on the ocean." The old man sighed once more.

"What's the name? Can you see the name of the boat?"

The old man looked up at Cody. "My eyesight ain't what it used to be. You want to have a look?" He nodded toward the machine.

"If you don't mind," Cody said. He leaned down and adjusted the glass to be able to see and then glanced up. Readjusting, he looked again at the boat bobbing in the water with its rear pointed toward the shore. *Big Tuna* it read. Cody huffed. He was out of ideas for getting Joey his money. Maybe he should just keep traveling. Going home could be dangerous.

"You're right, a nice evening," Cody said, walking away.

He'd travel down the beach a little way and see if he could doze on a park bench somewhere the police wouldn't shoo him away. Tomorrow, he'd have to find a way back home and talk to Joey. The weather was the only thing that was beautiful about the evening. His stomach rumbled reminding him he still hadn't eaten today.

He walked past campers and an occasional food truck, making his mouth water. Sometimes, late at night, they threw out food that hadn't been sold. He'd check back later. Sitting on a bench he leaned back and looked up at the stars as the sun slipped into the ocean in glorious shades of gold. Maybe the old man had been right. A night on the ocean could be what his soul needed.

A drunk tourist wandered his way swaying with a beer in his hand. He stumbled to the opposite end of the bench and Cody sighed. He'd hoped to be able to spend the night here, and now he had company. Instinctively, he moved as far to the other end as possible as the man fell onto the bench with a thud. His head bobbed twice and then fell back, his mouth ajar, and snored. The hand with the almost-full-beer-bottle beside him slowly fell away and it tottered on the seat. Cody reached to set it back up—no use spilling good beer—when he realized the bottle was still cold. The man had just purchased it. His mouth watered once more, and he took the man's beer and raised it to his lips.

"Cheers," he said and took a long draw on a beer that wasn't his.

The man continued to snore when his overweight body began to slide sideways. Without thinking, Cody reached for the man's shirt sleeve to pull him back upright when the moon came out from behind the clouds and shone on the polished leather billfold that poked out of the man's pants pocket. It was stuffed with bills. Cody looked around and realized they were the only two people on this end of the beach. No one would know if a tourist got drunk and lost his billfold. He'd just call his credit card company in the morning, and everything would be just fine. But tonight, he'd sleep on the beach.

Without another thought, Cody took the billfold and shoved it in his pocket, picked up the still cold beer, and walked away leaving the man to sleep it off. He strolled toward the other end of the beach with light, food and shelter. Tonight, he'd dine in style.

Chapter 9

Cody decided to spend the cash and leave the credit cards alone. Using them left a paper trail and, besides, the ID in the billfold didn't look anything like him. He wadded the cash into his pocket—the one without the hole—and tossed the genuine leather wallet in the closest trash can. He didn't want to be caught with someone else's ID.

He ate his fill at a taco stand and had a beer or two. He thought he should save as much of the money as possible and maybe use it as a downpayment for Joey. It might save his life. And anyway, he didn't need a five-star hotel. He didn't have the clothes to blend in. But a hot shower would have been nice. There were cabanas down the beach that sometimes were left up overnight and he'd use one to sleep in tonight. If he got caught, he could just say he drank too much and thought he was home. Act like a tourist.

He lay down on the slightly damp folding lounger that smelled like coconut oil and sunscreen. It had been left under the canopy though it probably should have been put away for the night. He looked out across the water. He could see a few spots of light probably from a fishing boat or something. Maybe he should try to get hired by one of them when this mess was over. He'd done some fishing when he was younger. His uncle was always trying to get him involved in fishing for a living.

It couldn't be that bad. He would be out on the water with a bunch of guys, not cooped up in an office or something. He could sleep on the boat when he was on the night shift. Like the old man at the dock said earlier today, there was nothing like being out on the ocean at night.

Tomorrow, he had to find his way back home and confront Joey letting him know he still didn't have all the money he owed. But for now, his stomach was full, and it was a beautiful evening. A cool breeze kicked up and he looked up at the stars. That was the last thing he remembered until someone shook him awake with the sun in his eyes.

"Hey, bum! Get off my chair!"

A young blond man in shorts and a clean tee shirt jiggled him awake. It was time to act like a tourist.

Cody smiled his most winning smile. "Hey, man. Where am I? Did I sleep here last night? Where's the girl?"

"I didn't see no girl, just you. She probably left. Now get up and out of my cabana. I need to clean it for the day."

Cody stood stretching and yawning in the morning sun. "I'm going. Hey, is there a bathroom around here?"

The cabana boy pointed down the beach and Cody headed that way. His belly was still full of tacos from last night and he slept on a lounger on the beach. Life was good. After taking care of the necessary items first thing in the morning, he needed to find his way back to Corpus and Joey.

He really wished he had some coffee and his toothbrush. His mouth tasted like stale tacos and beer. But it had felt worse. He could do this. He could talk Joey into giving him another chance since he had a downpayment on the money he owed. He'd done it before. He walked away feeling like he would live another day. Life was looking up after just the theft of one billfold. He was going to make it.

Cody walked back to the bus stop. The route wound its way along the coast to Corpus Christi. His worn-out tennis shoes felt every pebble in the road. It would be nice to own a set of wheels of his own. His uncle always said he didn't need a car, just a boat. It wasn't the only thing he and his uncle disagreed about.

When he climbed on the bus that was headed to the area where Joey's apartment was, he realized it was good to get off his feet. He dozed on the bus and almost missed his stop—a few blocks from Joey's apartment. When the big guy thumped down next to him in the seat, it jolted him awake. This was his stop. He yelled at the driver to wait and ran for the front of the bus barely getting through the doors before they closed and the driver once more proceeded on his intended route. No, he didn't want to be a bus driver with all those smelly people every day; a fisherman would be much better. He'd look into getting hired on a fishing trawler when this mess was over.

His feet once more felt the hard surface of the road as he walked toward Joey's. He would say he missed the job by just a few minutes, or he would have all the money. No, that sounded stupid. He could say he had the money but was robbed, or they didn't pay him like they said they would. Or he could admit to robbing some drunk dude. Joey didn't care where the money came from as long as he had it. He wondered how long he'd have to work for Joey to pay off his debt. And this time, he'd have to stay out of the product. Maybe he could convince Joey to give him another chance and leave his sister out of it. He had once been the best distributor Joey had in his operation, before he got into the stuff. He could do it; he could keep his hand out of the till, or his nose out of the product.

He had to.

As he approached the lot where Joey did his business, he saw Joey walking from the parking lot back into his dirty apartment. He looked pissed off as usual. Joey normally looked pissed off, so that wasn't unusual. Cody stopped, summoned all his courage, and walked that way. He needed to make this right. He raised his hand and waved but Joey didn't seem to notice as he walked into his apartment and closed the door.

Just as well, Cody thought. It gave him a little more time to think. He walked to the door of the grimy apartment and raised his hand to knock when the door opened and Joey stood there with a scowl on his face.

"Where you been?" he asked.

"The job on Mustang Island I told you about. But hey, they didn't pay like they said they would. I still don't have all the money, but I have some of it." Cody mustered up a smile that was quickly faltering no matter what he did. He stepped inside and closed the door behind him as Joey walked away.

When Cody turned, he saw a flash and felt a prick in the side of his bruised neck. Then a warm trickle began down his neck and into his shirt.

His neck. Again!

Without a word, Joey rushed him and shoved him once more up against the door. He pulled the knife from the wooden door and wiped the blood from it on Cody's shirt. It slowly dawned on Cody that the blood he saw was his and the knife was the one Joey was always playing with. This time he wasn't playing. How badly was he cut? His jugular vein ran through his neck. If it got cut, he could bleed out quickly. This guy was serious and really went for the throat! Cody reached up and held his hand over the wound as warm blood ran between his fingers. It was more than a bruise this time.

"I won't ask again," Joey said holding the knife up for Cody to see.

Cody reached into his pocket and pulled out the wad of cash. He had no idea how much there was. He had never counted it, but he had only spent a little of it. "This is what I have. I'll work off the rest. I think I'm going into the fishing business, and we can work out a deal. Maybe some of the fishermen would want to buy product. That would be a whole new group of customers to deal with. I will pay you, Joey!" Cody felt as close to crying as he had when his mother died.

Joey's eyes narrowed. "Yes, you will. And your sister will help."

Chapter 10

Dani had about given up on customers when laughter echoed from the shore. A limousine was stopped in the street. A gaggle of young women, in short skirts and high heels, stumbled down the dock with drinks in hand toward her boat. It was a little early to be drinking, Dani thought, then she saw the sash across the chest of the woman in a tiara that read "Bride." A bachelorette party. And they were heading her way.

"Hi!" the woman in the lead hollered as she waved. "Can we have a ride?"

Dani cleared her throat. "Of course you can have a ride. It is ten dollars a head. Do you need a tour of the island?"

The woman in charge whipped a credit card from the pocket of the severely tight dress she wore. From her shoulder hung a beaded bag as tiny as the dress so Dani wondered why the card wasn't in the purse. But maybe this was more convenient. Dani ran the plastic through her card reader and began pulling life jackets out of storage. She knew no one would wear one, but she'd have them available.

"Just find a seat anywhere. We need the boat balanced, so make sure not everyone sits on one side. Here are the life jackets if you want to wear one and we'll get underway in just a moment." There were more customers at one time than she was used to getting.

Dani started the engine of her tour boat. "Ladies, where are we going this afternoon?"

Dani performed her captain's duties explaining the safety precautions on the boat. No one listened. They weren't her first drunk passengers, not something she enjoyed, but she needed the money. And they weren't rowdy, yet. But as she toured the island pointing out places along the way, they seemed to become interested.

"I'm empty, and I need to pee," the bride announced turning her plastic cup upside down and dripping sticky liquid onto the deck of Dani's boat.

"Where's the closest bar?" asked the woman with the credit card.

"The Sneaky Teaky is right up here, and I can dock there if you like." Luckily, in the past few years, some of the bars had built small docks since running boats up on the sand was never good.

The woman once more pulled the credit card from her pocket. "We'll pay you double if you wait on us. We'd still like to see the rest of the island. Are there other places we'd like? Maybe a restaurant or something? And can we just leave our shoes on the boat since it's hard to walk on the sand in them?"

"Of course," Dani said with a smile as she accepted the card. This could turn into an expensive evening for the woman.

Dani watched the women walk down the small dock to the sand. Without their heels, they walked without wobbling. Maybe they weren't as drunk as she thought. The afternoon was ending and the waves on the water were becoming ripples. The women walked onto the patio of the bar and disappeared inside. The sun began to set slowly as Dani sat with feet up on the captain's chair, the sun behind her. It had been an eventful day with Cody, and now the wedding party.

It didn't take long before the women began filing off the patio with fresh drinks in hand and walking back to the boat. They'd found the bathroom and gotten refills to go. She thought she might direct them next to Le Chez's. They probably needed some food, and it was just around the corner.

"Everyone good?" Dani asked as they stepped back on the boat.

"I'm hungry," the bride announced as she took her seat.

Once more the bridesmaid in charge spoke up. "What's good around here?"

Dani looked up assuming the woman was talking to her. "Well, there is a nice restaurant up ahead called Le Chez. The food is great, and they have live music on the weekends—a jazz singer. Can I take you there?"

All heads nodded in agreement and Dani once more started the engine of the boat. Maybe there'd be a big tip in this if they liked the restaurant.

Le Chez had also put in a dock, and it increased their tourist trade. It was a small island, and the locals never worried about walking its length and width, but the tourists did. After pulling up to the dock, a young man in a crisp white shirt greeted the party.

"Good evening. Do you have reservations?"

"No, we didn't know we needed them," the bridesmaid said. "But she's getting married and we're having a party for her. Do you think you could squeeze us in just this once?" The woman with the credit card smiled demurely.

"I think we can do that," the young man said and

winked at Dani.

"I'll be here when you're finished," Dani called out and waved goodbye. The mixed smells of garlic and yeast wafted from the open windows, and she could hear music from one end of the building. Her stomach rumbled but she thought of the money she was making. It was a tradeoff. She wondered if she could get a glass of water and was about to leave the boat when the young man in the white shirt came down the dock with a tray in hand. It was covered in an equally crisp linen napkin. She wondered who had ordered food out here. She was the only one tied up at the dock. Then he opened the gate and stepped on her boat.

"Compliments of the chef," he said and quickly pulled the napkin from the plate handing it to her. "I hope you like shrimp scampi."

The plate held the most succulent meal Dani had ever seen. "I don't have much money at the moment. I can bring you some tomorrow," she said thinking of the cookie jar with its small amount of cash.

"No, you misunderstand. This is compliments of the chef. He wanted to thank you for bringing him the wedding party. *Bon Appetit*. Leave the dishes on the dock and I'll get them later."

He handed her the plate with silverware and a bottle of water. A dessert plate followed with a scoop of blackberry cobbler. This was the best meal she'd eaten since her mother died. She and Cody seldom cooked and if they did it was a boxed dinner.

When the waiter left the boat, she moved over to the seat for customers and sat with her feet up and the plate in her lap, the dessert plate beside her. After a long draw on the water bottle, she took a bite of shrimp and found herself drooling. Why had she waited so long to try this food? Sam was the chef's name, she remembered now. She chided herself once more for not getting to know her neighbors. She had overheard some Sandhill islanders saying he made the best yeast rolls they had ever eaten. She bit into the roll and discovered they were most definitely right. If she ate like this every day—like she could afford it—she would need a new wardrobe.

Wiping her mouth, Dani stood and belched loudly. She looked around to see who might have heard her, but she was by herself. Thankfully. Then she heard another sound. The most melodious voice she'd ever encountered began to sing "God Bless the Child" accompanied by a piano and bass fiddle. Could this evening get any better? A great meal and live music. Her mother used to listen to jazz on the old turntable that was probably still in a closet somewhere on the houseboat. Aside from that, Dani seldom heard music unless one of her tourists had a radio. Normally it was the music that accompanied some kid's video game as they sat on her boat.

She started to place the tray on the dock but thought she should take it closer to the restaurant. That would get her closer to the music.

Off to one side of the building was a covered wooden deck that hung with linen curtains blowing in the light, tropical breeze. That was where the music came from. Walking toward the deck she could see there were potted palm trees around the edge with the curtains that served as a screen. Placing the tray out of the way, she leaned against the pole that held up the roof and peered between the palm fronds. She could see a dark-haired woman in a long gold dress seated at the piano. A man in a Hawaiian shirt plucked the bass. He smiled at the singer as she sang with the most beautiful voice Dani had ever heard. So, this was the live music they had at Le Chez on the weekend.

"Beautiful, huh?"

Dani spun around, startled by the voice behind her. The waiter who brought her dinner stood behind her. He leaned down and retrieved the tray.

"I didn't hear you there. You frightened me. Yes, she's incredible. Who is she?"

"Billie Stone. She's from Sandhill Island originally. Grew up here. Then went to Corpus to become famous, lost her family in an accident and came back home. We're lucky to have her. How was the food?"

"Wonderful! The best meal I've had in ages. I really want to pay you for that."

"No, Sam said to feed you and maybe you'd come back and bring him more customers."

Dani smiled. "Maybe I can. I tell people about this place every time I tour the island. And I doubt he needs much advertisement."

"Well, your tourists may have over-indulged a little." The waiter nodded toward the restaurant. So, one of the women called the limo to pick them up here. I told her I'd let you know. And she said to ask for their shoes. She sent you this." He held out a wad of cash. So that was what the purse held.

"Wow. That was nice." Dani began to feel guilty about her original attitude toward the party. But she took the cash and shoved it in her pocket just as the lights of the limo pulled her attention to the road. "I'll get their shoes."

Dani walked back to the boat and picked up all the

shoes in the bottom of her vessel. She found five-and-a-half pair of heels that probably cost more than she made in a year. Where was the other one? Placing the stilettos on the seat she reached in the pocket on the back of the captain's chair for a flashlight. She hadn't realized how quickly it had become dark. She must have listened to the music longer than she realized. Down on her knees searching, she finally spied the shoe in the corner hooked on the leg of a seat. She pulled it from its prison to join the others on the seat and stood. Yes, there were six pair of shoes for six barefoot wedding guests.

Snatching up the shoes by the straps, she carried them down the dock to the waiting limo. The driver opened the back door where the disheveled women sat giggling.

"Six pair of stilettos, ladies," she said, handing them inside.

"Thank you!" they sang in unison and Dani stepped back waving.

"Good luck getting them home," she said to the driver.

"Oh, we'll be fine. It's not my first rodeo." The driver closed the door and Dani walked back down the dock to her boat. She turned and watched them drive away. Tourists. The island would collapse without them.

It was late. It was dark, and it wasn't until then that she realized she had missed the ferry home. Not only that, but she also had to negotiate the dark water back to her spot at the marina. It had been a while since she'd checked her running lights on *Wanderlust* and hoped they worked. It was late, and dark, but it had been a good evening financially.

Chapter 11

Joey knew Cody would never pay up. He had no way to make that much money. But his sister might and it was time to go straight to her. Even if she didn't have the money, she had the transportation. And no one would suspect her of being in the drug business. She was the perfect mule.

Now he'd see if she loved her brother.

He drove to the dock where she moored her houseboat. Most of the lights were out and people had gone to bed. But he knew—Jimmy at the dock told him—that she had clients late that evening. Jimmy had directed a bachelor party to her boat and kept her busy. He would have to pay Jimmy well, next time he saw him. He'd also confirmed she hadn't ridden the last ferry of the evening back to Corpus so she was probably out on the water. It was good to know she could navigate dark water. They could use that skill.

He pulled into the parking lot and stopped the car far enough away to not be seen. Even his dump of an apartment was better than this. Another fishy smelling dock. How people lived like this he had no idea. Parked away from prying eyes, they walked the rest of the way to the dock where the houseboat had been tied up for years.

The gentle lap of the water against the dock was the only sound they heard as they crept from the car to where

Dani's houseboat was tied. The lack of lights on inside the houseboat confirmed no one was home. Joey thought it was time to let Cody's sister know he was serious. If she didn't care about her brother, maybe she cared about her home.

The near moonless night would help conceal the operation Joey had in mind. He didn't need prying eyes when he sunk Dani's houseboat. They edged down the dock where the ancient vessel sat. Most of the lights were off along the way. Probably turned off for the night so the occupants of the slip could sleep in peace. But the lights above her houseboat shone brightly. Joey nodded to the flunky he brought with him then and looked up at the one dangling light that hung above the slot near Dani's boat. The man nodded back. What was the guy's name again? It didn't matter as long as he did his job. And he did.

The assistant held the shovel close to his body then lifted it to smack the bulb once. It shattered. Shards of glass fell onto the deck and into the dark water. It took a minute for their eyes to adjust to the darkness. Then they set to work.

Joey pulled out the hatchet hidden under his jacket and stepped onto the deck of the boat, then walked around to the opposite side. The axe would make short work of the aging aluminum pontoon.

Whack! Water splashed in Joey's face as the blade hit the pontoon cracking it open like a nut. The sucking noise from the gash started slowly at first and began to pick up speed. The shovel the other man carried came down with lightning speed on the bands that held the pontoon in place loosening it from deck of the houseboat. They worked in unison down the side of the deck, destroying the home Dani had inherited from her uncle and lived in most of her adult life. Quickly the punctured pontoon filled with salty water on one side and created a shift in the balance of the craft. It began to list to one side.

"Let's go," Joey whispered loud enough for his assistant to hear but hopefully no one else. The guy wasn't the brightest he had ever worked with, but he saw the danger in the shifting boat.

Stepping from the deck of the sinking vessel, Joey took several whacks at the rope that attached it to the dock and the craft leaned even more quickly as the underwater pontoon filled with water. Groans could be heard from the vessel as it succumbed to the briny deep waters.

Joey knew they had to go before someone else heard the commotion, and he signaled his companion to follow. They trotted down the dock back to the car in the parking lot and drove away before anyone saw what they did.

Joey looked back quickly as they drove away, "Let's see if this gets the sister's attention." If not, maybe he could destroy the other boat and the dock where it was moored. Hopefully, he wouldn't have to go that far for his sake and hers. He needed her and her boat for other purposes.

Groans could be heard from the submerging boat as it perched at a precarious angle before sinking and taking all of Dani's earthly possessions with it.

The man with the large floppy hat stepped out from the shadows of the dock and watched as Joey and his companion drove away.

Chapter 12

After the women were safely tucked in the limo, Dani walked back down the lighted dock where *Wanderlust* was tied, swatting mosquitoes as she went. She wasn't that far from the commercial marina where she needed to moor the tour boat—just around the tip of the island—but she had to get past the rocks and the tide was low. In the last few years, the island had installed lights on the rocks so vessels could avoid where they jutted up through the water. It was a godsend. Thankfully, she wasn't out after dark with her boat often. Fares or no fares, she didn't like being out alone after dark on the ocean.

Dani started the engine and tossed off the ropes that held her boat to the dock. The engine purred like a kitten. At least she wasn't low on fuel. She flipped the switch, making the forward and back lights glow a bright white. Red on the port side, left, and green on starboard, right, the running lights worked as they should. The dark water lapped on the sides of the vessel as she backed away from the dock. She was the only boat in the area to venture out this late that night. Sometimes there were party boats full of tourists, but not tonight. She had the island waters to herself. Pushing the throttle forward, thankfully, the breeze blew the relentless mosquitoes away. She hadn't taken the time to spray down with repellant.

Staying a good distance from the shore and the

rocks, she rounded the end of the jetty that stuck out into the ocean. Dolphins raced beside her boat even in the dark and she wondered if one of them was Scar. Waves sloshed once more pushing her sideways and she shoved the throttle forward steering away from the rocks. Better to be too far out than too close.

Once she'd rounded the tip, she could see the lighted marina and changed directions again. She'd check out her slip at the marina to see if she needed to do anything. Sometimes there were messages from the dock manager pinned to her slip. In the back of her mind, she thought of Cody and wondered where he was spending the night. She could sleep on *Wanderlust*, if it weren't for the mosquitoes, or just continue on home to Corpus across the strip of water that she traveled daily by ferry.

Pulling into her place she quickly saw that the marina was deserted. Even Poppy and his dog, Blackie, had gone home. Her lights shone on the pier where she tied up and there was no note there. She backed out and once more ventured into the black water. On the other side of the island was the route the ferry crossed, and it would get her home to her houseboat. She suddenly realized how tired she was, and the idea of a clean bed sounded wonderful.

She headed for the tip of the island. As she rounded the elongated strip of sand that had become a tourist destination in the past few years she found the island was asleep on this side near the mainland. There were a few tiki bars on the other side, but the ribbon of water between the island and the mainland was mostly deserted. Tourists and islanders alike had gone home for the night.

She looked at the ink-black water with a sliver of

moon hung above and was thankful for running lights. She followed the area that the ferry traveled during the day keeping away from any underwater cables and jetties. She'd grown up here and knew these waters, however they appeared alien in the night.

Unlike the island, the mainland never slept. The lights of Corpus Christi were visible even though the city was farther north. Most people didn't live on the ocean's edge. But she did. The marina where she tied her houseboat was west of the ferry's dock and she headed that way. The lights became dimmer the farther away from Corpus she traveled. Waves sloshed against her vessel reminding her that the ocean never slept. Its inhabitants were always in a fight for life, eating, fleeing, and procreating. Something large swam next to her and decided she was not important enough to engage tonight—and swam away.

Soon she could see the dim lights of the marina where her home floated. It was one of several marinas on this stretch of shore—and not one of the more affluent ones. She passed houseboats and other vessels tied up for the evening or permanently docked like hers. The lights seemed more dim than usual as she neared her slip. She hoped the neighbor's boat was still out for repairs, and she could tie up *Wanderlust* in his slip for the night. And she was right. It was not there.

That was when she realized the light that hung above her houseboat was out. She'd need to mention that to the landlord when she paid her rent. Slowing down as she rounded the dock, she headed to the empty slip next to her houseboat when she realized the dock and slip looked twisted. They'd been there for years and were routinely repaired as the salt water ate away at the moorings. But this looked like something had happened. Like a storm. But there had been no storms of late. She reversed the gears in the tour boat to slow her progress and then slid into neutral gear, floating as she studied the dock.

Something was wrong.

She could only see a part of her houseboat. The darkness of the marina didn't help, and she once again slid the throttle into drive to move the running lights closer to the houseboat. That was when she realized— the houseboat was only half there.

It sat at an odd angle partially submerged. Dani floated in neutral, her mouth ajar. Her home was underwater. One side had sunk into the ocean leaving the other side sticking up with one pontoon in the air.

Dani pulled *Wanderlust* into the vacant slip and quickly jumped out, tying off the vessel. Standing, she stared for a moment at the upended boat she called home. The more she stared, the stranger it looked. And then it hit her. Everything she owned was in that boat and underwater. Her shelter from the elements wasn't the only thing gone. So were her possessions. Her nice warm bed, the gun next to it for protection, the ugly green plaid sofa where Cody sometimes slept, and the cookie jar with her life savings (hardly anything) was underwater. She didn't even have a toothbrush or change of clothes.

"No!" she shouted to no one in particular. How could the universe do this to her?

Dani ran for the boat grabbing at its side scraping her hand on ragged pontoon metal as she snatched at the sinking vessel. As if she could really pull it back to the surface with just her bare hands. The door that Cody could jimmy when he wanted in was still closed. She stepped on the sinking pontoon, leaned forward and gently reached for the door handle with her bloodied hand. She realized her mistake when the boat groaned and sank deeper, taking her foot with it. She fell backwards onto the wooden dock scraping her bare legs leaving splinters in the back of her thigh. She couldn't retrieve anything. It was all ruined. Maybe, if she hired a scuba diver—with what money? Besides, they couldn't get in with their gear to retrieve the few things she owned. Her home was gone. It wasn't insured—who had that kind of money—and now she had nowhere to go.

She sat on the dock, bloodied and scraped as mosquitoes fed hungrily on her sweaty skin, but she didn't care.

How could this happen? What made the houseboat suddenly list to one side and sink? Did any of her neighbors see it happen? It was after 10:00, and many people were asleep or at least in for the night.

"Boat sunk, huh?"

She jerked around at the voice behind her. It came from the next slip over by a trash can. She could barely see a face and a large-brimmed hat. She stood wincing at the pain in her thigh where the splinters had sunk into flesh.

"What happened? Did you see it?" She limped toward the person in the shadows, blood dripping from her fingertips.

"Yeah, I might have. Two guys with axes. They did a number on your houseboat."

Dani squinted in the dark at the man behind the trashcans. "You saw them, and you didn't stop them?"

He shrugged. "There were two of them and I thought maybe you told them to do that. Stranger things have happened."

Dani seethed. "Of course, I didn't tell them to wreck my home. Are you crazy?" She looked closer and thought he looked like the man on the island with the broom. "You're the guy they call The Cleaner, aren't you? Well, Poppy calls you that."

"Yeah, Poppy. He's an original. Yes, that's what he calls me. You're Dani with the tour boat, right?"

"How do you know my name?"

"It's a small island."

Suddenly Dani felt nervous. Who was this man and how did he know so much about her and Sandhill Island? Her hand ached and the splinters in the back of her thighs stung. The mosquitoes seemed to have disappeared or was she just so miserable she no longer felt them?

"Dani?"

She heard a voice heading her way down the dock. It was Carla, her neighbor who came and went on weekends.

Dani turned and faced the woman. "Carla, did you see this?"

The woman marched toward her in the dark with a man following behind. "We heard noises earlier and thought maybe you were home. And then Ned looked out and said he couldn't see your boat or your lights. What happened?"

Dani didn't know Ned and Carla well. They only lived here on weekends. Actually, she knew very few people here on the dock since she was seldom home, working daylight till dark.

"I think someone sunk my houseboat and knocked out the light in the process. This guy said…" She turned back where The Cleaner had stood, but he was gone. She twirled around. "Did you see that guy in the big floppy hat that was talking to me?"

They shook their heads.

And it hit her like a boulder; she had nowhere to even spend the night, except onboard *Wanderlust.* "Everything I owned was on that boat." A single tear slipped over her lashes and down her cheek. She hadn't cried since her mother died. She didn't know she still could.

Carla slipped an arm around her shoulder. "Well, honey, we have a couch, and you are welcome to it as long as you want, isn't that right, Ned?"

Ned nodded. He was obviously a man of few words.

Dani stood still as Carla attempted to pull her toward their weekend boat and looked around. "I just can't believe it. The guy in the hat said he saw two guys with axes sink my home. And he didn't try to stop them. Why?"

"Well, sweetie, we didn't see anyone. We should call the police. But I think things will look better in the morning. Why don't you come get some sleep at our place tonight?"

Almost against her will, Dani left her boat as it sank farther into the dark water. She knew she could do nothing for it, but still felt she should stay. But she was exhausted, and the couch Carla mentioned sounded wonderful. Maybe she could find some tweezers to remove the splinters too.

Chapter 13

Dani woke with a start realizing she was not in her home. She'd slept on Carla's couch and was covered in a thin blanket. She still wore last night's clothes except for her shoes which were on the floor. Her hand was bandaged, and the backs of her thighs still ached.

Sitting up on the edge of the couch, she ran her hand over her head and then rubbed her eyes. When Carla tiptoed into the kitchen and pushed the button on the coffee pot, she glanced at Dani.

"I'm sorry, did I wake you?"

Dani stretched and attempted a smile. "No, I just woke up. Believe it or not, I slept like the dead. I didn't think I'd sleep at all." She stood and realized her legs would still hold her even after the devastation of last night. Carla had helped her remove the splinters before bed. Her home was at the bottom of the ocean. She guessed she was lucky not to be trapped in it. And the scent of coffee crawled up her nostrils. She breathed deeply. Was this what addiction was like? It was possible she was addicted to caffeine.

Carla smiled. "Well, I'm glad you slept. You were so upset. We all were. I can't imagine how that boat just sank."

"Well, according to the man they call The Cleaner, it had help, two guys with axes. Though I can't imagine why." And then she thought of Cody and his buddies.

Maybe it was a message to her that she had to help them with drug delivery. She had told them no, a thing she hadn't thought of until now.

Carla pulled food from the fridge. Soon she was cooking breakfast when her husband came from the bedroom in a robe and slippers. Carla kissed his cheek and handed him the first cup of coffee.

"Dani?" she asked as she filled another and gestured toward the pot.

"Oh, please," Dani said without thinking.

Carla handed Dani her coffee and pulled a pan from under the stove, then cracked eggs into a bowl. "And I'll have some breakfast ready shortly. Don't even think about saying no. Then you can have a shower and plan your day. You've had quite a scare."

Carla didn't seem like someone to argue with once she set her mind to something. Dani folded her bedding and moved it to the end of the couch by the door. The table was close enough to the couch and her bed would be in the way of breakfast.

After Carla's wonderful breakfast and the use of their shower, Dani emerged in a tee shirt and shorts that were too big for her but aside from what she slept in, the borrowed ones from Carla were all she had. She stuffed the wad of cash from the wedding party in her pocket and folded up her dirty clothes into a bag Carla had given her.

"Now that couch is yours as long as you need it. We go home during the week, but you are still welcome even if we're not here." Carla said with a hug as Dani walked out the door.

Dani knew she couldn't impose for long, but she thanked her anyway. With a goodbye, she walked down the dock to where *Wanderlust* was tied. The morning sun shone on the water where her houseboat had sunk the night before. Dani stood and stared at the spot where her home had been for years. How could this happen? Why?

Carla had reported the destruction to the police, and they were on the crime scene early. There was probably no need to come last night. But at least they were investigating.

Dani hung around long enough to answer the questions from the police. They all asked the same thing; did she see anything. The answer was no, she wasn't there until after 10:00 and the deed had already been done.

"If we're finished here, I need to get to Sandhill Island. I tie *Wanderlust* up there for the tourists. I may be coming back here to sleep for a while, but if you need me, you can find me on the island."

Chapter 14

Back on Sandhill Island, the day was hot and still—much like the customer base she'd seen all day. Hot for the new water taxis that were taking the tourists from her by storm. Still like her boat that sat tied up to the dock.

She constantly thought of the houseboat and wondered what had happened. She didn't have insurance, so replacing her home was impossible. She could stay with Carla for a while, but the gas for *Wanderlust* back and forth from the mainland every day would eat a hole in her budget. She needed to find a place to live on Sandhill Island. There were furnished apartments available—since she no longer owned anything and she wouldn't be paying rent anymore for the houseboat slip. At least after the sunken vessel was removed. How the hell would she be able to afford that? She'd have to worry about that later. She had no idea how long she had to remove the houseboat from the dock.

Dani pulled the insulated lunch bag Carla had packed from under the captain's chair and contemplated its contents: Ham and cheese sandwich, chips, and an apple. The water in her to-go cup was long gone. Even with the cover over the boat, the sun would eventually move enough to beat down wherever she sat.

She plucked the sandwich from the plastic bag and munched. It remained cool due to the freezer pack next to the food. She stared out at the gentle waves on the water as she ate her lunch. Tossing her trash back in the lunch bag, she walked down the dock to find something to drink.

Reaching the end of the dock, she walked toward the downtown area. The small town catered to tourism and had recently built wooden sidewalks in front of the stores. An ice cream shop had been open summers for the last few years, and she thought about how refreshing the cold concoction would be. They would probably give her water to go with an ice cream cone. That appealed more than anything all day. She opened the door to the artificially cool shop and soaked up the air conditioning.

"Come in out of the heat, Dani. We hardly ever see you. You want something to cool you off?" The woman behind the counter stood with curly auburn hair pulled back in a clip. Her young face was a myriad of freckles across a pert nose. She offered a friendly smile, and Dani remembered her name was Sienna.

"Hi, Sienna. Yes, something cold. How about a Rocky Road in a cone and can I get some water?"

"You bet. Have a seat." Sienna scooped ice cream into a ball and pressed it into a cone. It occurred to Dani that she never really interacted with her neighbors since she sat on the dock daily waiting on customers.

Sienna brought the cone and a cup of water to the table. Dani looked up from her view of the window at the end of the building's oceanside view. "We were really shocked to hear about your houseboat. Poppy said it was sunk. That's terrible."

Dani was stunned. "I guess everyone knows about my house."

"Yeah, and we're really sorry." Sienna nodded

toward the water. "Tide's low today. You can see the strand of sand that is forming on the windward side of our beautiful island. It's getting bigger all the time. I love to walk on it when it's this visible. I know they'll dredge it out someday when it becomes a problem for the boats."

Dani nodded and slurped the frozen cream, picking out the nuts and chocolate to eat them first. She gazed out the window that probably had to be washed daily from salt spray. Wiping her mouth with a napkin she sighed. She seldom gave herself any time off. The ice cream was a real treat. She stood and looked around for a trash can and picked up the cold ice water in the cup.

Dani glanced at Sienna. "Well, my customers are scarce. Maybe I should go wading."

"You should. You can go out a long ways before you even get your shorts wet."

Dani smiled as she stared out the window. "I think I will. I'm taking a little time for myself today. Thanks for the ice cream and cool air."

Sienna wiped the counter as she called back. "Any time. Come back and see us. And good for you, taking some me time for yourself."

Dani pushed the door open with one hand, the cup of water in the other and turned to look at the ocean. It was always there like a trusted friend. It had mood swings, but it was eternal, and Dani liked that.

She wondered if she was in shock today. What happened last night completely changed her life and she wasn't on her tour boat hustling customers. Staring out to sea, she walked toward the area where she thought the famous sandbar had begun its new life.

Suddenly a shadow loomed over her, and a tall, dark-skinned man rounded the corner nearly running into her.

"Pardon me! I almost ran you over. I seem to have my head somewhere else today," the man said as he backed up.

Dani looked up at the tall lanky man and felt a blush begin on her face. "No problem. I wasn't watching where I was going."

He took off his sunglasses and extended a hand. "Alfred Stringer," he said with a wide smile. His dark skin accentuated dark brown, almost black, eyes. "I live upstairs. Well, at the moment. I'm moving. You own that tour boat tied up on the dock, *Wanderlust*, right?"

It was hard to keep a secret on the small island. "Yes. Danielle Brown. Everyone calls me Dani." She smiled and stared at those dark eyes.

"They call me String. You headed out to the beach?"

"I thought I'd investigate the sandbar that is developing. I hear with the tide out it is a good place to avoid with a boat. But maybe a nice place to wade. Sienna, in the ice cream shop, says you can wade out a ways without getting your clothes wet. I wanted to try."

"Well, she should know. She and her boyfriend are always out there. He makes maps of the ocean floor and has been warning all the boat owners. Most of the people who live around here know about it, but some of the vacationers don't."

"Yes, the Snowbirds sometimes get into trouble on the ocean. Do you play bass fiddle at Le Chez with another singer? I saw you last night."

"Yes, that's me, unless I was out of tune last night. Then it was someone else."

"I don't know much about music, but the two of you were wonderful. I just heard a small amount. I had a tour and had to get back. But it was lovely."

String placed his sunglasses back on his face. "Thank you. Come hear us again. It was a pleasure to meet you, Dani. I hope to see you again. Enjoy that sandbar." He nodded and walked away toward the other end of the island.

It wasn't until he walked away that Dani looked up and realized he had come down the stairs from above the restaurant. There must be an apartment upstairs.

****

After watching String walk away, Dani strolled toward the water. String, what a nice man. And attractive. She found she was still thinking of those dark eyes, when she realized she was at the water's edge. There was the strand that the waves had built in recent months. It hadn't been an active season yet, but storms were on their way and who knew what Mother Nature had in mind for their little island.

She kicked off her shoes and walked out into the cool water. She had no idea how cold the wave was until it hit her hot skin. It refreshed her like the ice cream. It felt better than anything she'd felt in the last twelve hours. First her feet disappeared and then slowly her legs as they were covered with water. She sipped from the cup as she walked, and slowly the ocean came closer to the edge of her shorts. Then the sand began to drop off and Dani knew she would be getting wet if she continued on. With her hand up to shade her eyes from the sun, she looked into the distance when she saw the dark triangle of a fin headed her way. A shark. They sometimes came into shallow water to feed.

When she turned around to head back, she was astonished to see how far out she had waded. Glancing back at the approaching fin she tried to run through thigh deep water but made slow progress. How stupid to think she was safe because she could stand. She knew the ocean better than that. She was no tourist.

Twisting around again, she realized there were two fins, and one was coming from the other direction. She ran as fast as her legs would take her when she heard a splash. Without thinking she looked back and fell face first into the ocean, sunglasses tumbling. She pushed herself up with the help of her hands and once more raced for shore as fast as her legs would take her through the water.

She glanced back and realized the shark fin was going the other way just as she heard a familiar series of whistles. Scar! He swam past and she wobbled in his wake. Rolling onto his back, belly up, he smiled his dolphin smile and once more squeaked at her.

"Scar! You ran the shark off. You saved me!"

The dolphin appeared to wave as he once more headed out to sea. She trotted to dry land and almost stepped on her sunglasses as they washed up sparkling in the sun. Reaching down, she placed them back on her wet face and walked off toward where she left her shoes. She had no idea where the cup went. It would end up polluting the ocean like all the other plastic.

The shark was like another omen of things to come: first the sinking of her home and then the near-death experience with the shark. Thank God for a friendly dolphin. She wasn't a superstitious person, but life was not normal these days. What would make it seem normal was some customers. It was time to get back to work—thanks to Scar she was still alive to do that.

Chapter 15

There were few fares that day due to the heat, so Dani quit early. She had just been going through the motions all day. No wonder the customers were passing her by. She was going to have to find a place to live, and she'd seen at least one apartment about to become empty. Why hadn't she asked String about it? Maybe Poppy could tell her who owned the apartment above Le Chez. He knew everything and everyone. He had been sitting in his usual place on the other end of the dock, so she walked that way.

He waved. "Afternoon!"

Poppy fished almost daily at the same place. Dani wondered if he ever caught anything or if he just sat there watching the world go by. "Hello, Poppy." She waved back at the man who always looked homeless to anyone who didn't know him or didn't live on the island. Poppy was a long-standing citizen of the island. He was always ready and available to help his neighbors. Dani had heard he was sometimes taken care of by Meg and Jon Stanford and the trust they maintained. Many on the island were. Dani didn't accept charity. At least, she never had. She earned her way in life.

Poppy sat in the shade of the building on the dock with a faded green hat on his head and his faithful dog, Blackie, by his side. Poppy told Dani that Billie Stone had given him the dog when he helped her take care of its mother and her litter of pups.

"Blackie, how are you this hot afternoon?" Dani held her hand up to her eyes and looked in the direction of the pair who sat on the dock most days. The dog smiled a doggie smile. He made her think of Scar, the one good thing that had happened to her today.

Poppy waved and then spoke. "Hi, Dani. I was real sorry to hear about your houseboat sinking."

Dani's mouth dropped open. How did he know about her boat? "My houseboat? How did you know about that? It took place just last night in Corpus Christi."

Poppy shrugged. "People talk. Good people and bad people. I just listen. But I'm real sorry."

Dani stammered. "Well, thank you. It's very kind of you to say that."

"I guess you don't have a home now. That makes me sad."

"Well, I have a place to stay tonight and for a short while. But I need an apartment or something. Do you know of any that are vacant? I know it's summer and rentals are probably full. I talked to Alfred Stringer this morning and he was moving from the place above Le Chez. Do you know who owns that?"

"String? He's a nice guy. He sings with Billie at Le Chez. He's moving to a beach house down the way."

"Yes, that's what he said. Who did he rent from; do you know?"

"Yeah, I know."

There was a pause.

"Well, does the chef at Le Chez own the apartment?"

"Yeah, I think so. String lived up there and sang on

the patio at the restaurant. I don't know why he's moving. Bigger place I guess. People are always wanting a bigger place. Don't make no sense to me."

"Okay, thank you. I'll talk to the chef. What's his name?"

"Sam. Gives me fish sometimes. And he's a good cook, too."

"Sam," she said. She waved goodbye and walked toward the restaurant. She could smell the garlic cooking as she got closer.

She walked to the back of the restaurant and found there was a small herb garden. A man in an apron leaned over picking herbs and placing them in a basket.

As she was about to approach him, a faded blue compact car drove up and parked in the restaurant parking lot. String pulled empty boxes from the trunk and headed to the steps of the apartment above the restaurant.

"Leaving us?" the man picking herbs called out to String.

"Almost empty, boss." String called back. He looked Dani's way and waved. "You're not out on the water? Too hot?"

"Hi, String," Dani said. "I was hoping to see you." As soon as the words left her mouth, she blushed. "I mean I wanted to talk to you about the apartment."

He smiled. "Nice to see you, too. Hey, I heard about your houseboat. I'm so sorry. Did they catch the guys who did it?"

"Does everyone on the island know about my houseboat already? It only happened last night."

"News travels fast on a small island. Especially bad news."

"Well, the police have no leads. I was thinking about the apartment you're leaving. Is it rented? And can I afford it?"

The man working the garden stood and stretched his back. "I'm Sam. I don't know if we've officially met before. Thanks for bringing that wedding party to my establishment last night. We can always use the patrons. Like String said, I'm so sorry to hear about your houseboat. I hope they catch the guys who did it and find out why. But I'm planning to rent the apartment as soon as I can get it cleaned. You want it? Utilities are included."

Dani paused. She wasn't used to paying rent for an apartment. It would probably be more than the rent to tie up the houseboat, but she no longer had that expense. "I don't know if I can afford it. I haven't paid rent in a long time."

"Well, we can haggle about that. It's furnished and I guess you need that. String here normally cleans up after himself pretty well so I doubt it's too dirty. He just got a nice beach house on the other end of the island. I guess he wanted more room. But I'd just like to keep the apartment full so it's taken care of. If you want it it's yours. And if you have trouble making rent, I could always use help in the kitchen on clean up duty. Why don't you plan to move in as soon as String is out?"

Dani didn't know what to say. She could help out at the restaurant at night. She seldom had night tours. "Well, you know I don't have a regular income. It depends upon the tourists and then there's wintertime." She paused. "But I'd be happy to help out in the kitchen anytime I don't have fares. I normally don't have tourists at night. Last night was unusual."

Sam smiled. "Then it's settled. You move in as soon as String is out, and it will make us all happy. Glad to have you as a renter and employee, Dani Brown."

Dani realized she didn't have to introduce herself. Everyone knew her name and her dilemma of late. And she also realized she had just rented an apartment. Now she had to pay for it.

Sam stuck out his hand and she stared at it for moment—then she shook it. "Thank you. I'll take good care of it, and I'd be happy to help you whenever you need me." She could not believe her good luck.

Dani turned to String. "I could help you pack if you like."

String smiled and handed her a box then pulled a few more from the trunk. She followed him upstairs.

It was an efficiency apartment—all one room with the kitchen on one end and the bedroom and bathroom on the other. The sofa was in between. The bathroom and closet had the only doors except for the front door. The windows faced the ocean and there was a small deck at the top of the stairs near the front door.

"It's small, but it worked for me," String said as Dani looked around.

"It's probably more room than the houseboat."

After String left with the last load of boxes, she sat on the edge of the bed and looked around. She could make this work, especially with the second job.

Then it hit her; the bed had no sheets. She didn't even have towels. Everything she ever owned was at the bottom of the ocean. The gravity of the situation began to sink onto her shoulders when she realized she could take a shower but had no towel to dry with. All the money she had in the world was in her pocket and she had to make it last. The cookie jar with the small amount of cash she had saved went to a watery grave with the rest of her things. Tears welled up in her eyes, again. One minute she was happy, and now this—when someone knocked on her door.

She jumped—and then walked to the door wiping away the tears. String had probably forgotten something.

Opening the door, she found the same server who brought her dinner last night while she waited on the wedding party. He worked for Sam at Le Chez.

"Sam asked me to invite you to dinner. He says he won't take no for an answer. Employees eat free. It's a perk. And it's Tuesday so the special is flounder. Oh, and Meg sent this box of things over. I told her I'd deliver it to you. Where do you want it?" He set the large box on the floor.

Dani realized she hadn't said a word. She stood with her mouth open, but nothing came out. She nodded to the box. "Meg?"

"Meg Stanford. She owns most everything around here. It's her big house with the garden that provides most of the produce Sam uses. Anyway, she thought you might need a few things. She heard about your houseboat sinking. We all have. We're very sorry." He pushed the box farther inside the door with his foot. "Sam says come whenever you're ready."

He left and she wondered if he even heard her squeak out "thank you."

She was invited to dinner downstairs at the restaurant. The only thing she had to wear were the clothes she wore into the ocean that day. And they weren't even hers. She couldn't go to the restaurant looking like this. Starting for the bathroom, she stubbed her toe on the carton that sat next to the door.

Opening the box, she found clothes, toiletries, sheets, and towels. And in the bottom was a container of coffee to go with the pot that String left for her on the counter.

This time the tears fell, and she was afraid they might not stop.

Carrying the box to the bed, she pulled out shorts, jeans, tee shirts, underwear, and even a sundress with matching sandals. She knew Meg, having bought her jam, and had heard of the Stanford Trust, but she had to thank her. She even knew what size Dani wore. She held the dress up to her and looked in the only mirror in the place in the bathroom and smiled. Maybe her luck was turning around. She needed to call Carla and tell her the good news. She had a place to stay.

Grabbing the towel and soap, she headed to the shower. This day was getting better. And she loved flounder.

Chapter 16

Dani stepped through the door of the restaurant and inhaled the aroma of food. Good food, not like the TV dinners she sometimes cooked. The sundress itched in places where she wasn't used to having fabric and her hair was blowing around her. She opted to leave it down for a change—but she found herself blowing it out of her face. Her days of shorts and tee shirts on the boat had spoiled her. She could hear music coming from the outside deck when the server appeared at her elbow.

"Dani, I'm glad you came." He smiled as he gestured toward the deck. "Sam said to give you the table in the back so you can hear Billie tonight. Next time, you'll probably be working."

"I'm sorry, this has all been so quick, I didn't get your name."

"Aaron. I'm Sam's nephew and I'm home for the summer. I always help him during break. He needs all the workers he can get, and I need a summer job."

"Well, Aaron, thank you. This is all so surprising. I'm used to being out on the water, not in a restaurant as nice as this. Your uncle has been very kind."

Once on the patio she was seated at the back. She could hear String on the big double bass as he accompanied the woman at the piano. Their voices melded like smooth caramel and Dani stared in awe at the talent. Her hard days on the water had taught her nothing about music, but she knew she was in love with the sounds coming from the stage. She sipped from the water glass on her table when Aaron arrived with a basket of rolls.

"Sam makes the best rolls I've ever eaten," Aaron said as he set them in front of her.

Another waiter arrived with her salad and a glass of wine. "Sam suggests the flounder. It's local."

"That sounds wonderful," she said and realized she was being slowly seduced by the music and food. She took a drink of the wine. Normally a beer drinker, she held it up to the light of the setting sun to admire the golden glow. She could forget her problems with evenings like this.

The entree arrived just as String began a solo.

After dinner—and there was dessert—she stayed at the table until the pair quit singing. The crowd was small. She didn't think her table was needed.

As she drained her wine glass, Sam arrived. He carried a wine bottle and refilled her glass without asking then turned the chair around and faced her across the table.

"So how was it?" Sam smiled as he poured himself a glass of the golden liquid.

"That is the best meal I've ever eaten. Better than my mother used to cook and certainly better than I can do. Thank you so much. I hope you didn't need the table. I was just sitting and listening to the music."

"No, it's fine. Glad you enjoyed it. You deserve a break. By the way, the Stanford Trust is taking care of your sunken vessel. Meg said not to worry about it."

Her mouth fell open. Meg again, she thought. "I have to talk to her. She's done so much for me."

"Well Sandhill Island takes care of their own. Now tomorrow night we'll probably be busy. I'll need you in the kitchen. Wear your jeans and come prepared to work. Dinner will be on me again. Employees eat free. Get here as soon as you can after the last tour. We open at 6:00."

Dani agreed as Sam stood to leave. String waved at the pair after putting away the instruments and mics, then walked to the table.

"Great job as always, my friend," Sam said patting String on the shoulder and walked back to the kitchen.

"Your music is wonderful," Dani said.

String broke into a large smile. "Thank you. I'm glad you came. Billie never misses a beat. We've been together for many years. She's why I came here. We just work well together. How's the new apartment? I hope things are clean."

"It's great. Meg sent over a box of things I hadn't even thought about. Everything I owned ended up underwater. I didn't even have clothes, or linens. But things are looking up. This meal, and a job…and some new friends." She smiled at the man in front of her and took a long sip of wine. Was she flirting? She doubted she even knew how anymore. It had been a long time.

"Well, let me walk you home," he said as she drained her glass.

"It's just upstairs."

"I know exactly where it is, but a gentleman doesn't let a lady see herself home."

He pulled her chair out as she stood and they walked off the deck, into the sand.

"I am so full," she said as she rubbed her belly.

"A little walk on the beach before you go in?"

She nodded and they walked away from the

restaurant down the beach. She quickly got sand in the sandals and reached for his arm as she pulled off the shoe.

"Sorry," she said pulling her hand back.

He smiled. "Here, let me help you. Or better still there is a bench over there."

She nodded and they walked to the bench. After sitting, she took off the sandals and brushed the sand from her feet.

String cleared his throat. "So, Dani, are you from around here? I grew up on the mainland and have only lived here a little while."

"Originally from Corpus. I bought the *Wanderlust* and began to charter trips after my mom and uncle died and I inherited the houseboat to live in." She sighed. "The one that's at the bottom of the ocean right now."

"Yeah, I'm sorry about that. It must have been hard. But I hope you'll like the apartment. It's small but the views are magnificent."

"I think it will be good for me. It will save a lot of time running back and forth from Corpus. So, have you been a musician all your life?"

"Well, yes, I guess. I don't know anything else. I grew up with a bass fiddle. My mother was an orchestra teacher, and I guess I was drawn to the bass immediately. Actually, I started on cello and guitar only because I was too small to pick up and maneuver the bass. But she taught me to play any stringed instrument as well as the piano. But I loved that bass! I remember fingering the thick strings when I was a child in Mom's school room. I could feel those deep tones all through my body. Still do."

Dani's eyes followed String's as he looked out to the

ocean watching the lights of a shrimper floating by. "You come by your love of music honestly," she said.

Taking a deep breath, String began again, "I guess I do. But I always met Mom in the orchestra room after classes were finished. I credit her with teaching me to love music. But she always warned me not to knock over the giant fiddle. It was worth a lot of money, she said, and she could not afford to buy a new one. The school only had one bass fiddle and someday it would be mine to play."

Dani looked into his eyes and even in the dark she could tell he had a lot of love for his mother.

"Mom was also a great lover of music. And she taught that love to her students. She pressed me to live the life of a musician—not a teacher like her. She said I had the talent to make a living doing what I loved, and she didn't want me to be tied to the constraints of a school board and the lessons she was forced to teach. She'd say, 'Ally, you're a free spirit and I want to watch you soar.'" He chuckled. "I guess I believed her."

Dani watched his face and could see not only his love for music, but his mother. "So, she called you Ally?"

"Ally or Alfred when I was in trouble. String came later in the smoky bars and stages playing music to a lot of drunk crowds. But I guess I made a name for myself in the jazz district and made my momma proud. I've been doing it ever since. Mom was right."

"So, when did you start playing bars?" she asked.

"Before I graduated high school, I was playing in the Corpus Christi jazz district on the weekends late at night. Not of legal age, I was often paid under the table after being let in the back door secretly. At least I got paid.

That is where I got the nickname String after the bass I played and of course my last name, Stringer."

"So, is that where you met Billie Stone?"

"Yeah, one evening before our set and before the crowds came in, this dark-haired woman in the gold dress walked in looking out of place, and kinda nervous. I think it was her first time in that bar. No one in the band knew her, but somehow she managed to get an audition. She walked to the microphone, adjusting it to her height like she was putting off the inevitable and opened her mouth. It was love at first sight." He smiled. "Not romantic love, she was more like a little sister, but it was love and we became friends. She had the voice of an angel. When she crooned into the microphone, the crowd stood still. She didn't just sing into the microphone; she was the microphone. She became the music, and it flowed in and out of her like the instrument she became. And I had a sister for the first time in my life having been an only child.

"Anyway, we were doing well, and I guess you could say becoming famous together in the Corpus Christi jazz scene playing and singing together. Then tragedy struck. Her family was killed in a head-on collision by an idiot going the wrong way. After her hospital stay, she came home to live with her mother who was also ill, and she contacted me. She had a gig at Le Chez on the weekends, did I want to join her?

"I followed her here because I loved to make music with her—and to make sure she was safe. She'd been through enough. Not more than a year later, the idiot who killed her family was back and causing trouble. He spent time in jail, and he thought she should help him once he got out. That ended badly for him. Don't ever make

Billie mad."

A wave rushed in as Dani saw two lovers walking hand in hand in the moonlight. "So, you moved here from Corpus?"

"I already lived in that apartment when her trouble began. The man who killed her family went back to jail again, as he should have. And recently, Billie told me about a beach house that was available near her. I could still walk down the beach to work in the evenings and maybe I'd take up fishing during the week. I'm determined to learn to cook for myself and quit living off taco stands during the week. I always have plenty of good food from Le Chez on the weekends.

He sighed and looked at her. "Anyway, that's me, the long version. How about you?"

Dani looked out to sea and wondered how much she wanted to tell him.

"Well, my mom and dad lived in Corpus and had two kids at a young age. I was the oldest. My dad left us, and my mom raised us. My uncle was a fisherman with his own fishing boat, and he lived on a houseboat. Always at sea. My brother and I grew up there as much as at home and we learned to love the ocean, and he taught us to fish. He and my mother died at about the same time and I stayed on the houseboat and bought the tour boat for excursions on Sandhill Island. My brother is in and out of my life, he's not very reliable, but I love him. And that's about it, I guess. Here I am living in your old apartment, taking tours during the day and washing dishes at night to make ends meet."

She covered her mouth with her hand to hide the yawn.

String smiled. "You must be tired, and I talked too

much. How about we finish that walk home."

She nodded as she stood, and they walked back toward the restaurant and apartment behind it. They rounded the corner to the stairs that led to her new home.

Once at her door, he turned and faced her. "I'm glad I met you, Dani Brown. And I know Sam is glad to have you helping in the kitchen and occupying the apartment. I'll see you tomorrow." He walked away with a wave.

She watched as he headed toward his new home. Things were looking up. Yes, her home was at the bottom of the ocean, but she had a new one—and new friends—and even a new job. Well, a second job. She was still the captain of *Wanderlust*. But now she'd have an additional paycheck to help out. Yes, life was looking up.

After she put the sheets on the bed and was stuffed full of the best meal she'd ever eaten, she thought about all that had happened in the last twenty-four hours. How would she be able to sleep in her new place? Dani was certain she'd toss and turn for hours, and she had to get up early to catch the tourists.

And with thoughts of String and the music still ringing in her ears, she quickly fell asleep in her new bed.

Chapter 17

The front door rattled. Then a quick click.

Dani snapped awake. Acting on instinct, she reached for the drawer of the bedside table for a gun she no longer owned. She had a sick feeling of deja vu.

"Sis?"

Cody again? She climbed out of bed in her pajamas and walked toward the door confused at first as to where she was.

"Cody? Is that you? How did you know where to find me? And why can't you come in the middle of the day like everyone else?"

She flipped on the light.

Cody stood at her front door. Brown shaggy hair in his eyes, he looked at her and winced in pain. There was a bandage on his throat which was an even deeper color of purple than when she saw him last.

"Hey, sis." He lurched forward and she thought he was drunk again, until she saw the man with greasy black hair behind him. He had shoved Cody forward.

As the sleep left her eyes, she realized the man had a gun at Cody's back.

"What the hell?" she said as she reached for her brother.

The man with the gun waved her away.

"Dani, this is Joey," Cody said as he was shoved roughly toward the sofa where he sat with a plop.

Joey's smile matched his hair, and he looked Dani up and down, the gun pointed toward her. "So, you're Dani. Cody has talked about you. And I understand you have a boat. Well, one anyway. It's a shame what happened to the other one."

Dani bristled and then stared at the man's gun, then her brother. "Cody, what happened to your neck?"

"Nothin.' It's no big deal." He tried to smile again.

"No, Dani," Joey began. "It's no big deal. But I have a big deal for you."

Dani nodded at the gun pointed her way. "If it's no big deal then why the weapon? I don't like it pointed at me or anyone else for that matter."

Joey smiled then lowered the gun to his side. "Okay, it's not pointed at you—right now. But I have a business deal for you. Your brother owes me big time and has no way to pay me back. Well, he has you. And you have a boat. And I need some product transported out in open water. I get the product to you on Sandhill Island, and you transport it to the boat that will meet you out to sea. Easy peasy. You do this for me, and your brother's slate is wiped clean. He says you want to keep him alive."

"Of course, I want my brother alive. But I am not transporting drugs for you."

"Yes, you will." He pointed the gun at Cody who sat on the couch. "If you want your brother alive—and I think you do."

Cody's eyes became large, and he shrank back as Joey cocked the hammer.

"Stop!" Dani took a deep breath while stepping forward. She had to fix this. "How much money does my brother owe you? Maybe I could pay off his debt."

"You got a spare six figures on you?"

Dani's eyes mirrored her brothers. He owed the dealer six figures? How could he end up in debt that far? What had he done? "No, I don't have that much money. In fact, most everything I own went down with my home today and I'll bet you know something about that."

"Your houseboat? Oh, that's a shame. But I don't think it was worth the amount of money were talking about here."

Dani had no idea how much the houseboat was worth, but it was trashed now. Maybe she could get a loan from the bank, but they'd want collateral. "No, I don't have the money you need, but maybe I could get a loan."

"No, no banks, no police, just a business deal between you and me. I let your brother live and you transport some product. You can buy the gas."

"Please sis, it's just this one time and I'll help you with your business after that." Cody looked at Dani with pleading eyes. "I don't want to die."

Dani looked at her brother and thought of the little boy who followed her around when he was a kid. What would Mom do? And she opened her mouth regretting what was about to come out before it even left her. "Okay, one time. I transport once for you, and you leave Cody alone. That's the deal. One time and only one time."

Joey took his eyes off Cody and slowly turned his head toward Dani. He released the hammer and lowered the weapon to his side. "You really do love this little addict. Not sure my sister would do that for me."

Dani mumbled that she doubted she would either, hoping he didn't hear.

"All right, one time. And we'll see how well you do

your job." Joey waved the gun toward Cody gesturing that he should follow. "But for now, Cody comes with me. You'll find the coordinates for the boat you're meeting on your tour boat in the morning." He reached for the door and nodded to Cody. "Tell your sister you'll see her tomorrow at the boat."

Dani reached for her brother, but Joey grabbed Cody by the arm and pushed him toward the door. "No, he goes with me for now. See you tomorrow."

Chapter 18

Dani tossed and turned until she finally saw the glimmer of pink in the east. Yawning, she stretched and sat up. Breakfast was the last thing on her mind, but coffee could come in handy today.

Coffee brewed while she brushed her teeth and dressed. It might be the only good thing in her life today. She took the commuter cup to the deck of the apartment and looked at the lights in the direction of the dock.

Dani needed to get her boat fueled and ready. It was too early for tourists. She hoped her fuel tank was big enough to hold the amount of diesel it would take to get where she was going and back again. Her boat was not meant for extended trips on deep seas. She grabbed her hat and sunglasses, and walked out the door of her apartment leaving it unlocked. She didn't own much these days and String didn't give her a key. Why would a locked door make her feel safe anyway?

She walked down the long dock toward *Wanderlust* tied up in its slip. The boat was moored with its rectangular front tied to the wooden dock. There were bumpers on either side preventing it from sloshing into the piers that separated each slip. It rocked back and forth in the gentle morning waves. There on the seat meant for customers was a bag with a piece of paper stuck underneath.

Pulling the paper out she read the coordinates and

stuck it in her back pocket. She slid the bag under the captain's chair. No need to look inside. Let's get this over with, she thought. Instinctively, she started the engine and pulled around to the pumps.

"Mornin', Dani. Need any help with that?" Jimmy, the attendant who worked in the marina was normally not chatty. Why today, she wondered? But her luck was running out if today was anything like last night.

"No, Jimmy, but thanks." She always pumped her own gas and today would be no different. She stood longer filling the seemingly endless tank, knowing it wasn't really endless, however open water was at least three miles out from shore. She had no idea where she was going after that. She hoped her little GPS would guide her. She seldom used it.

"Wow, more fuel than usual," Jimmy said with a smile and handed her a small bucket of shad for Scar. It was the morning routine.

"I won't need that this morning," Dani said just as Scar arrived at the side of the boat with good morning clicks and whistles. She smiled and realized she hadn't smiled since the incident with Joey last night. "Well, maybe I do." She dug deeper into her pocket. She doubted that Scar would follow her today, but his company might be just what she needed. After paying, she tossed a fish to Scar and then headed back to her slip on the dock.

Pulling into her place, Dani left the engine idling and the boat sat untethered in its slip. Deep in thought she tossed a fish to Scar. There was no way out of this. After today she was a mule for a drug dealer, and it was all the fault of her baby brother. The one she would die to protect.

Just then, Scar did an acrobatic jump into the air to get her attention. She tossed him a fish which he caught in midair then splashed down drenching her. She wiped her sunglasses on her tee shirt and smiled at the dolphin. She hoped to see him again.

She backed *Wanderlust* from its moorings.

"There will be more fish in the deal for you when I get back," she said as she backed away from the dock. This would be a one-time deal. One time. And then her brother would be safe. And he'd go to work for her. She'd go into debt for another boat that he could captain. It would be worth it to have him unharmed even if it weren't a good business decision right now.

Cody was worth it.

****

As soon as Dani left, Jimmy called the number Joey had given him. He was to report when *Wanderlust* left for open water. It didn't take long, and it made some money. This could be easy and financially a good thing. And he wasn't hurting anyone. Why did he care what Dani was doing or why.

He stood looking out to sea when a boat pulled up.

"Fill it for you, sir?" he said as the man tied the boat so it would not float away from the dock.

"Yep, might as well fill it all the way up. I'll use it eventually."

And Jimmy was back to his normal day, filling the boats of his neighbors and tourists. Yes, working for Joey was a good idea. So was getting off this island and doing something else.

Chapter 19

As she moved across the water, Dani stared at the magnificent sunrise shining between clouds. She was surprised she even noticed. The pink shades of the sun bounced off the water. "Red sky at night, sailors' delight. Red sky at morning, sailors take warning." Her uncle always quoted that old saying and now she was faced with a pinkish color to the sky. Not red but getting close.

Red sky or not, she needed to get going. Taking a deep breath, she headed out away from the security of the dock and her life. She had no idea how to manage what she was up against. She didn't own a weapon anymore and that was probably best. It might be used against her and Cody. But she was sure the dealers would be armed. She'd have to rely on her intellect to get them both out of this alive. Her uncle would say this was a problem that was like being between the devil and the deep blue sea. The sea she knew. Cody's devil was a stranger to her.

Hearing a splash, she looked to the left and saw Scar was keeping up with her by jumping and diving like the pro he was. She smiled in spite of herself.

She checked the coordinates on her little GPS and pointed *Wanderlust* in the direction she had been given. At three miles out, she would no longer be able to see the island where she lived. The deep water was different out that far. You could easily lose your bearings and she didn't know how to navigate by the stars.

When she got to the place she was to meet the other boat, she throttled the engine back and surveyed the horizon. She was to meet the speedboat here and she didn't see anything around her. They were fast. Fast enough to outrun the police and certainly fast enough to outrun her. Was she early? Or were they planning to make a grand entrance. Those boats were quick and maneuverable, unlike W*anderlust*. She knew they could appear out of nowhere.

And it did.

From the west she saw a shiny pinpoint heading her way. An orange spot grew larger as it sped in her direction. The spot became an elongated orange cigar that sped across the water like greased lightning. The sun bounced off it and she raised her hand to shade her eyes even with her sunglasses and hat on, as it glittered in the early morning sun. She wondered why they didn't use some kind of ocean camouflage, maybe in a dark blue with white waves painted on it. But who was she to tell a drug dealer how to paint his boat.

The boat circled her once then stopped, sloshing water over her deck. She tried not to get knocked over by their waves and grabbed her chair hanging on while she desperately looked for her brother on the other boat. And there he sat in the bottom. He either was knocked out of his seat by the speed of the boat and the waves it took or was down there to hide. It didn't matter. He was alive and that was enough for her. Now to get both of them home alive.

"Hey, pretty lady captain. How are you today? I have your brother. Do you have my product for me?" Rodriquez asked.

****

Rodriquez was the captain of his own ship, even if it was a cigar boat. It wasn't his, but he was the captain. The cartel handed him a job and a boat to do it with. They even gave him a couple of men to help him out. The boat was fast and could outrun most everything on the water. And the fast boat could flip upside down if not piloted in a proper manner. He knew that. Hopefully, he knew what he was doing.

Rodriquez was from Mexico where the only jobs available were with the cartel. He had no family, so he was only concerned about himself—and that was by design. He knew not to try to have a regular life and deal drugs. The cartel had him by the balls and they squeezed whenever they wanted to. But it was a paycheck. A good paycheck and one he intended to keep coming in. It didn't matter what he was told to do; he could make it happen—even if he disagreed with it.

And this time his bosses were right. If they could get a local to bring them the product out far enough no one could see what they were doing, they could move twice as much as they had by land trying to avoid the cops.

This tour boat was just what they needed. And the captain was a woman. Even better. She could be easily maneuvered. He had a way with women. They always did what he said. And if they didn't, he could be persuasive in other ways.

Chapter 20

Joey was nowhere on the boat. Dani wasn't sure why she thought he would be, but these men were all strangers. She was away from shore with people she didn't know and running drugs for them. The two occupants in the boat with her brother looked as greasy and dirty as Joey. They could have been his twins, but Cody's dealer wasn't there. Maybe that was good and maybe it was bad. What had she gotten herself into?

The dealer who talked to her smiled and showed signs of tooth loss. Did he use his own product or just not brush his teeth? She doubted he'd be dumb enough to use the drugs he sold. But Cody had.

Cody stood as best he could with the waves created by the speedboat and attempted a smile at his sister. There were dark circles under his eyes and his hands shook. He needed a fix. Or maybe he was just nervous. They both had good reason to be.

Dani cleared her throat. "I have it. I'll give it to you as soon as my brother is on board my vessel."

A line was quickly thrown over her railing and the dealer jumped on board with her tying the two boats together. He smiled when she jumped. She wasn't doing a very good job of appearing calm.

He reached out a hand for the bag.

"No, Cody gets onboard my boat first."

"I call the shots here, lady captain. I am in charge. I

will say when your brother moves to your boat. Now where is my product?"

Dani glanced at Cody who nodded his head as if to say give it to him.

"Cody, you okay?" she called to the other boat.

"I'm good, sis," he said his voice shaking.

Against her better judgment, she bent over and reached for the bag under the captain's chair. She held it out for the dealer to take and he took it from her hand. She was officially a drug dealer now, she thought.

"Okay, you have it. I'm leaving now and my brother goes, too." She leaned forward and reached for the line to untie the two boats when her hand was stopped by one much larger and stronger than hers. This was not going to end well.

"Leave my sister alone!" Cody shouted though his voice shook.

The man on Dani's boat pointed a finger at Cody. "You, junkie! I said sit down. I'll tell you when you can talk, and it isn't now."

Cody looked at Dani with pleading eyes and then sat in the seat like a little boy who had just been scolded.

Dani stood back up and eyed the man who had tethered the two boats together. What did he want from her? "You have the drugs. Now Cody goes with me back home and this is all over and done with. I told Joey one time and one time only." She spoke, hopefully sounding much braver than she felt.

"And you did a good job, lady captain. And you will do a good job again next time. Your brother's life depends upon it."

Dani seethed. But what did she expect from these ruthless thugs? "No, the deal was one time. You got your product and Cody and I will leave now. Don't contact us again." She reached her hand toward her brother to help him change boats but was shoved roughly back.

The other drug dealer tossed a similar bag to Rodriquez on board her boat, and he handed it to Dani. She assumed it was payment for the drugs she had delivered.

"You, and you alone, will take this bag back to the island. Joey will be waiting to meet you where you dock. If you go somewhere else and don't arrive on time he has been instructed to burn down your little dock and send it to the bottom, just like he sank your houseboat. Your services are still needed. And your brother stays with us until we are done with the both of you." He pulled his phone from his pocket and started to dial. "What do I tell him? Should I say that the lady captain is cooperating, or should he take out your dock and all your neighbors' boats?"

Dani glanced at Cody, who looked like he was about to pass out. When was the last time he'd had food or water? If she left him with the dealers he would surely die. "You don't seem to be taking very good care of your hostage. That is my brother and the only reason I'm here. When was the last time he ate or drank? Give him water now, or he's leaving with me." She had no idea how she was going to make good on that threat, but it was worth a try.

The first man who had been doing all the talking looked at his partner and nodded toward the small ice chest in the boat. The partner reached in and pulled out a bottle of water, handing it to Cody. After a moment of struggling to open it, Cody turned the bottle up and drank thirstily.

"And something to eat. It's hot out here and he's dehydrated, but he needs food too."

"I have a banana and a mango," the other man said, holding them up for the thug in charge to see. The man still on her boat nodded. Cody reached for them greedily and peeled the banana then shoved half of it in his mouth at once.

It wasn't much, but at least it was something.

"Take the bag to Joey and you will receive further instructions from him."

Dani stared at her brother and wondered what would happen if she left. But what choice did she really have?

"I'll take the bag to Joey, and I want to talk to my brother when I get there. He can't live on fruit. He needs real food. Besides, what good is a dead hostage to you anyway? You'd feed and water a dog, and he's not a dog."

"Give the bag to Joey and he'll tell you what to do." The thug nodded his head, and he pulled the tether from the boats as he jumped into the speedboat. He sat and the partner quickly hit the throttle knocking Cody to the side. He was lucky he didn't fall out.

Dani rubbed a hand across her eyes. This was not what she expected. Cody was supposed to come home with her. And now she had to run drugs again. She placed the new bag between her feet as she sat in her captain's chair, started the engine, and turned toward home. Suddenly she hated her life on the water. The one that had felt so freeing, being her own boss. She looked forward to doing dishes for Sam at Le Chez. At least she hoped she still had a job there. If this morning were any indication, her life could take any turn at any moment.

Chapter 21

Joey's cell rang just as he was handing out the product to the regulars who always showed up in the morning. It was Rodriquez, his contact with the cartel. He shoved the last of the addicts away and turned his back to answer the call. They could wait. He didn't want to miss this call.

"Hello." He tried to sound casual. If this job worked out with Dani and Cody transporting the stuff, he would be on his way to the big time.

The gruff voice on the other end cleared his throat. "She's on her way back. Be at the dock to meet her. And make her believe you will burn the place down if she does anything stupid."

"You got it, boss," he said and clicked off. He had to get to the Island and make Cody's sister think he was serious. She loved her little island and the boats that docked there. She'd do anything to keep her lifestyle, her brother, and the people of the island safe. At least he hoped so.

****

Dani knew she had to act normal when she got back to Sandhill Island. Joey would show up and he'd take whatever was in the bag. It was probably cash, she wasn't going to look. Then she needed to be prepared to work at Le Chez tonight. Hopefully, no one would ask why she left early and came back without customers.

Three miles back home might as well have been
three hundred. Her mind was racing, and she had no idea
if she'd ever see her brother alive again. How did she get
into this mess? Well, she knew how—it was Cody and
his habit that caused this problem. But she couldn't think
of that now. She had to stay strong for both of them. She
thought of contacting the island police but knew if Joey
got wind of it, Cody would die. She was better off alone.

Sooner than she thought she saw the dock at
Sandhill Island. Three miles wasn't that far. There
wasn't a lot of activity on the dock in the middle of the
day. The big tour boats were already out on the water.
She was missing fares. But that was a small problem
right now.

Pulling to the dock she throttled back and rounded
the corner where *Wanderlust* moored. She could see
Poppy at the end of the dock in his normal place and she
waved, trying to appear nonchalant. She coasted into her
slip and tied up the boat. She'd left at the crack of dawn,
and it was now after lunch. Suddenly she was hungry,
and it made her think of her brother. She wondered if
Cody had eaten by now. Wasn't he supposed to call her?

A man dressed in black with a baseball cap and
sunglasses walked her way. Something about his
presence made her nervous and she looked away. A
shadow appeared in front of her as he climbed in her boat
without a word. He took the sunglasses from his face.
Joey. Here to pick up the bag. Someone must have called
him.

"You have something of mine?"

Dani slid the bag toward him with the tip of her toe.
She didn't even want to touch it.

Joey, reached down, unzipped the top, glanced in,

and quickly zipped it back up. He pulled his phone from his pocket and touched a button. "It's here," was all he said.

"Hey," Dani said. "My brother was supposed to call me to let me know he's eaten."

"She wants to know about her brother." Joey smiled and hung up, placing the phone back in his pocket. "He's munching on tacos right now. Wish I was with him."

Then looking at her closely, Joey said, "I'm here to pick up the package, and to let you know that if you don't cooperate, you won't be the only one to suffer. You and your brother—and the whole town—will find out what happens when you cross us. It would be a shame if your little dock should burn down. Your neighbors would probably blame you." He turned and walked away down the dock with the bag in his hand.

Dani's heart was racing. Who saw that? Who knew Joey on the island, and did they think she was involved with him? She was, whether she wanted to be or not. She glanced around her and the only person she saw was Jimmy at the pumps looking her way. But he always saw her as she came and went. She would ignore him.

Her stomach growled. She'd go to the grocery store and pick up a few things for her fridge. How she could be hungry at a time like this, she had no idea. Then after a sandwich, she would come back and wait for tourists. It was important to look normal at a time like this. And she needed the money from washing dishes.

The tiny grocery store on the island just had the basics. Most people went to Corpus for the bigger items. But she was able to get some drinks, bread, and sandwich makings. She bought granola bars for breakfast. Her toaster was at the bottom of the bay along with everything else, including Meg's blackberry jam. At least she had a coffee pot and coffee, thanks to Meg. She had to talk to her when this was all over and thank her for her kindness. Assuming she survived.

She paid for her items from the roll of money in the pocket of her shorts and walked out the door with several sacks in her hands,

And ran into String.

"Hey," he said with a smile. "How's the apartment? Are you getting used to being on dry land?" He reached for her sacks, and she gave him half of them to carry. Something about him was so easy. They walked side by side toward the apartment they'd occupied.

"I fell asleep almost immediately. Of course, it might have had something to do with the huge meal Sam fed me. I can't get too used to that."

"He is a tremendous cook. So, you start work this evening?"

"Yes, I got some groceries and then thought I'd go back to the boat to wait for a few fares before my shift this evening. I think I'll enjoy the change of pace." She hoped she sounded as casual as she tried. "How about you? Are you liking your new place?"

"I'm kinda rattling around in it. I didn't have much to move and now I need to buy some furniture. The previous owners left a few things, but once I get settled, I'll decide what else I need. You should come see it once I get everything put away. It's on the other end of the island by the rocks where everyone likes to fish. Billie told me about it when it went up for sale. It's over by her."

"I'd like to meet her. I didn't have time last night. What a voice. Both of you. I am amazed at your talents."

She thought he almost blushed.

"Well, I'll try to introduce you tonight, if you're not too busy."

"I'd like that. Well, here's my place…But I guess you knew that. Thank you for helping me carry the load."

He smiled and nodded. "See you tonight. Have a good afternoon."

"Thank you," she said thinking that was exactly what she needed. She climbed the stairs and opened the door to her apartment. She plugged in her cell to be sure it kept a charge. She needed to be available for any calls about Cody. She put the groceries away and then made a sandwich. She needed to get to the dock and make things seem normal. This was not going to be easy.

Chapter 22

The sun beat down on her boat, but she sat in the shade with the sandwich and the commuter cup of water—which still tasted like coffee. She paced the small boat or sat tapping her foot. Anyone who saw her would wonder why she was so anxious. The afternoon coasted by and finally a family of four showed up for a tour. The money could come in handy. She had no idea when Le Chez would pay her. She didn't think to ask.

She gave the family her normal tour and then brought them back to the dock. "Thanks for riding with Island Tours and enjoy your stay on Sandhill Island." She hoped her voice sounded more upbeat than she felt. Tourists told other tourists of their experience. It was late in the afternoon, and she put away the life jackets and headed to her apartment for a shower and change of clothes. She'd eat dinner at Le Chez whenever Sam told her. It had been a long time since she'd worked for someone else. But she planned to clean the kitchen to the best of her ability and be a good employee. Sam deserved it. And it would help pay the bills and keep her busy.

Downstairs from her apartment was the back door of Le Chez. It was unlocked and she hoped this was how she was supposed to enter. The kitchen was already a bustle of activity. Rolls sat on the counter ready for the oven. An assistant chopped salad greens and dishes were stacked ready to be heaped with food and placed in front of customers. Desserts were cut and left to chill in the coolers.

"Dani, how was your day on the water?" Sam said as he hustled by with fresh herbs gathered from his ever-growing garden. More produce lay in baskets ready to be washed and used.

"Good. Not a lot of fares, but that's okay. Where do I need to start?"

Sam ladled a small amount of red liquid into a bowl and thrust it at her—then handed her a spoon. "First, I want you to sample the tomato bisque made from Meg's fresh tomatoes and tell me what you think. Enough spice?"

Unused to gourmet food, Dani wasn't sure how to respond until she tasted it. She raised the spoon to her lips. The soup slid down her throat and reminded her of tasting her grandmother's tomatoes still warm from the sun. Homegrown tomatoes were the best. As a child she would bite into them and let the juice run down her face. She resisted the urge to wipe her hand across her mouth like she had as a kid. "This is wonderful! Oh, so good." Food like this could make her forget her troubles—maybe. "No, the spice is perfect, not that I'm an expert. But as a customer, I'd love it."

"That's what I want to hear." He placed the ladle on a spoon rest. "Let me show what I need you to do. The dishes are clean from last night and we place them here on this rack for use. That won't last long on a Saturday night. As soon as we have clean ones, place them here. We have two dishwashers and one or the other will be running most of the time. The pots and pans have to be scrubbed in this sink. The gloves are here along with the soap and scrubbers. And check the trash in the kitchen now and then. It will need to be taken outside when full."

Dani was never one to spend a lot of time in the kitchen, but she could understand when something was dirty and when it was clean. But she needed instructions on how to operate the dishwashers since she'd never had one. Sam explained it to her.

She nodded her head. She understood what needed to be done. And she was glad to be busy until she received her next set of instructions from Joey. It would make the time go faster.

Glancing up, she saw the first customers come in the door. It wasn't long before she could hear music in the distance, but she was too busy to go look. She was certain it was Billie and String.

The hard work was good for her and made her forget her troubles. She barely thought of Cody all night. Barely. Sometimes he crept into her head. But she kept him at bay so she could keep her mind on washing the dishes for Sam. She needed that apartment and the money to pay for it. She couldn't afford to lose this job— or her brother.

As quickly as it started the rush was over. The last customers wandered outside, and the music ended. Both dishwashers hummed as she scrubbed the last pot and wiped it dry. She had no idea where Sam kept them when they were not in use.

"Good job, Dani," Sam said as he came into the back where Dani wiped down the counter tops. "Did you get a chance to eat?"

"No, I was too busy. I'll do that next time," she said taking off her apron. She still had not heard from Joey. Her cellphone remained quiet in her back pocket. He hadn't said how he would contact her, just that he would.

Sam handed her a sack with Styrofoam containers. "Here's some pasta—I think you'll like it. And there's a cup of the tomato bisque. And since blackberries are in season, I added some cobbler." He smiled as he handed her the prize she wondered if she'd be able to eat. "And Shayla is outside waiting to talk to you."

"Shayla?" she quickly wondered if she was involved in this mess too, or maybe she wanted to know where Cody was. What could she tell her?

"I think she has something for you. Thanks for helping out and we'll see you again tomorrow night if you can. Let me know if you get tied up."

"Thank you," she said wondering what Shayla could want. She walked to the front of the restaurant and out the door. She found her leaning up against the post at the front of the parking lot.

"Hey, Shayla," Dani said trying to sound casual. "Sam said you were waiting on me."

Shayla smiled and stepped toward Dani, then quickly hugged her. "I'm so sorry about your houseboat. I thought you might need some things, and I was cleaning out anyway. So, I left a bag at your apartment door. Nothing big, just a little this and that. How's Cody? I haven't seen much of him lately. The last time I saw him, I took him to the bus. He was going to Mustang Island. Had a business deal or something. I hope he's doing okay."

"Yeah, he's fine." Dani lied. "I saw him yesterday." She knew she was starting to sweat, and it wasn't the weather or the hard work this evening. "But thanks for asking about him." She started to walk away.

"He's using again, isn't he?"

Dani turned back around not knowing whether to be

irritated that everyone knew her business or pleased that they took an interest. "Yeah, I'm sorry to say he's using again. I don't know what to do for him. He always wants to borrow money and never wants to work. I hope to get him into rehab soon." That was true. If he survived this latest catastrophe, she would get him into rehab one way or another.

"Well, let me know if I can help. I really do care about him and wish him—both of you—the best." She turned and walked away leaving Dani with her dinner in hand.

At the top of the stairs sat the trash bag Shayla had brought her. She carried it in with her dinner. More evidence that the people of Sandhill Island cared about each other.

****

Shayla walked toward her car and waved at Poppy. He was just leaving the dock and heading for home. He, too, had a sack with dinner from Sam. The chef's food never went to waste. He fed anyone who needed it.

"Hi, Poppy. Did Sam give you fish?"

"He is always good to me. I didn't catch anything today. But Blackie and I always eat thanks to Sam."

"He's a good guy. Have you seen Cody lately? I'm a little concerned about him, and Dani hasn't seen him. You know everyone around here. Have you seen him?"

Poppy shook his head. "No, but he always shows up. Dani has been working hard with her tour boat and working for Sam, too. She left really early this morning and was gone for a long time."

The Cleaner stepped out of the shadows and nodded at Shayla. She jumped. "Do you know where Dani went early this morning, Poppy?"

Poppy looked surprised to see him too. "Shayla, this is The Cleaner. I call him that because he cleans stuff around here."

The man in the large, brimmed hat and broom nodded at Shayla.

Shayla eyed him carefully then cleared her throat, "And who are you? I've seen you around lately. It's a small island. Poppy isn't the only one who knows everyone."

The Cleaner looked off in the distance and the back at her. "Yeah, I'm just passing through. I'm enjoying the weather and the beach. But I've gotten to know Dani since she's always around. I was concerned about her too."

"I'm sure she will be fine." Shalya turned to go.

The Cleaner reached for her arm, then stopped before touching her. "Well, it's not a good thing for a person to go out alone on the ocean with no one else around. Just concerned is all." He tipped his hat and disappeared into the shadows.

Chapter 23

From the back seat of the black SUV with darkened windows, Cody saw a sign that said he was back in Corpus Christi. He'd seen the seamy side of Corpus before, but even he hadn't seen this part of the city. The dingy motel room at least had a bathroom even if it was filthy. The toilet might have been cleaned years ago. The shower drained slowly, though he hadn't had a shower in a while and probably wasn't going to get one. But he heard the dealers complain about it. He couldn't have cared less if it drained or not. If he could just feel the warm water running down his head, it would be a blessing. But that would not happen.

If drug dealers made so much money, why were they staying in a dump like this he wondered? And he thought of Joey and his nasty apartment. If Joey had the money to stay in the Ritz Carlton, his room would still be filthy. He was just that kind of person. He might shower once a week and as far as housekeeping went…well, it didn't. He would never let someone else clean his place. He wouldn't let them in, and they couldn't get it clean if they tried. It was as simple as that.

At his own apartment, if the landlord came knocking to inspect, Joey would probably be evicted. If the landlord cared. Joey probably didn't rent a place where the landlord cared about anything but the rent. If Joey were a landlord, he'd be the same. He would give new meaning to the word slumlord. Cody would remember never to rent a place like where he was tonight. If he lived to rent anything, that was. He'd rather sleep on the beach. It was cleaner, the air was fresher, and the views were spectacular.

He had no idea why he was concerned about cleanliness at a time like this. He was about to die, if Dani didn't come through, and maybe even if she did. He might die if he didn't get a fix soon, but he doubted it. He'd only wish he could die.

These thoughts were floating through his mind when supper arrived. The delivery guy had probably been to this motel room many times since he seemed unconcerned about anything but his tip. He handed the greasy sacks through the door and then the drink container came next.

"Thanks," he said as he backed away counting his money. He climbed into his aging car, which needed a muffler, and lit a cigarette as he sped away to the next stop. The car backfired as he pressed the accelerator. It might have needed more than a muffler.

"Junkie," one of the dealers shouted. "Get your supper now or I'll eat it!" Cody grabbed the food that was handed him and sat on the floor to eat. He devoured it like it was his mom's Thanksgiving feast. Hunger would make you do that. Then he laid his head back against the dirty wall and closed his eyes for a moment.

The tacos were cheap and greasy but welcomed. He couldn't remember when he ate last. But the tacos and the sun had made him so thirsty he couldn't get enough to drink. Or maybe it was the lack of drugs that dehydrated his body. He refilled his drink cup with water from the bathroom sink that left a taste in his mouth he couldn't identify, and he sipped slowly this time. It might be the last water he had for a while. He looked around the room.

He wondered if the health department knew about this place. If he got out of this alive, he would tell someone. He had no idea why he cared. If he lived, he'd never be back. But the motel and the delivery driver would go on the same. Life was like that. If he died tomorrow, it would continue just the same. It was a daunting thought but a realistic one.

Cody heard the men speaking Spanish and caught enough to know they weren't going back out tomorrow. They were waiting for the word as to when they would meet Dani again. He wondered what drug dealers did when they weren't dealing drugs. And he almost laughed to himself. He was a drug dealer. Not a successful one, but he'd dealt drugs just the same. He knew what he would do. He'd wait until called. And so would they.

And the headache hit, followed by chills and sweating. He rolled over in a ball onto the floor and stared sideways at the TV game show that continued day in and day out. How did people watch daytime TV? He was going through withdrawal symptoms in a dump of a motel room with daytime TV. To pass the time, they played cards on the table in the room and passed around a bottle of tequila that he wouldn't even get a sip from. He remembered once crawling to the bathroom and drinking from the filthy faucet once more. It tasted awful, but it might be what kept him alive.

The room had two beds and a couch. They were equally dirty. When he fell face forward on one bedspread, he was certain he saw movement on the fabric just before dozing off—only to be kicked and told to move to the couch. He didn't really care as long as he could lie down. The couch was probably better than the floor.

He had been a long time without a fix and the minimal food and water were taking their toll. He was exhausted and who knew when he might be able to rest again. The couch smelled like the last guy who slept there—or the last fifty—but he fell asleep anyway knowing he could be awakened at any time to once more meet with Dani. But it was his stomach that woke him up. He was hungry again. He hoped his captors were too and would order something soon.

The TV blared day and night, and the card game continued. The dealers passed out for a while, ordered more food and tequila, played more cards, and Cody tried to stay alive. He ate when there was food and lay on the couch or floor the rest of the time. He couldn't die. What would they do to Dani if he weren't there? They needed him to be alive to keep Dani coming back.

He heard they were going out again in a few days. This time late in the day. Having lived near the water, Cody knew how quickly it became dark on the ocean even with a full moon and that made him even more nervous for himself and his sister. The endless watching of card games and bottles of tequila passed around along with daytime TV were his only companions. But at least he was eating.

Cody dreamed of tacos chasing him down grimy alleys and people yelling and kicking him—when he realized someone was kicking him. The dealer who told him to sleep on the couch now insisted he get up. It was time to go. Surely he hadn't slept all day. Then he saw the sunset sky as the door opened and he was shoved roughly out to the car.

****

Dani sat on her tour boat and watched daily as tourists came and went. She washed dishes for Sam and waited on instructions from Joey—mostly she worried about her brother. Where was he and was he alive.

Maybe she should call the police. Maybe she should tell someone—but what would she say? She had nothing to tell them, no GPS coordinates to follow, no idea where to start finding her brother. If Joey came back, or notes appeared on her boat, then she would have something to say. She'd wait.

Chapter 24

Days went by with no contact from Joey or the drug dealers. Dani had no idea if her brother were alive or dead, but she was certain they would contact her again to run drugs for them. She tried to act like her life was normal.

She sat on *Wanderlust* daily waiting to see if there were tourists who wanted to tour her island. But they were in short supply. Sometimes she would walk down the beach just to stay busy and tour her little island from dry land. One day she walked a little farther, past the place where she waded out into the water and was chased by the shark. Then she continued.

In the distance she could see the large house that sat near the water with the pillars out front holding up the roof to a beautiful porch. She could never imagine living in a house like that. She knew it was Meg Stanford's house, and she also knew she owed Meg a thank you for the clothes and things she sent over to the new apartment when Dani had nothing.

She could see someone in the back yard tending the vegetable garden in a faded sundress and ragged straw hat. She knew it was Meg. She'd never been to her home, and maybe it was time to pay Meg a visit. She walked to the front of the house and then along the path uphill toward the figure in the garden.

She waved as she got closer. "Hi, Meg!"

Meg waved back and stood stretching her spine.

"I saw you out working and wanted to stop by to thank you for all the clothes and things you sent over after the houseboat sank—or whatever it did." She stepped closer and looked at the woman in front of her. Her gardening clothes were worn out, but the woman appeared radiant. Dani knew that Meg was old enough to be her mother, but she looked happy and healthy. Maybe it was Alex who made her that happy.

"You are very welcome. You deserved it. I was happy to help. Oh, would you like some blackberries? I have so many they are going to go to waste." Without waiting for an answer, she trudged up the hill motioning Dani to follow.

And she was right. Near the top of the hill were the blackberry plants, some on trellises and some growing on bushes. They were loaded with berries to the point some were brushing the ground from the weight. Meg handed her a basket and they both began to pick the ripest and juiciest of the group.

"I want you to know, my son, Jon, has a company that will be pulling out your houseboat tomorrow."

Dani's mouth dropped open in surprise. "Sam told me you were doing that. I don't know how I would have accomplished that alone. Thank you—again!"

Meg stood with a smile and handed Dani the basket of berries. "We take care of each other on Sandhill Island. I don't know if anything is salvageable, but you might want to be there if you can."

"Tomorrow? So soon! I was afraid it would be there forever. Thank you again. I'll be there," she said as she took the basket. "Again, I don't know how to tell you how much I appreciate your help lately. Maybe I can help you with this garden sometime to pay you back."

"If you have a spare moment, that would be wonderful. But you need to show some tourists our home." Meg smiled.

Though she didn't know her well, Dani had never known anyone like Meg—unlimited funds and she used them to take care of her neighbors. She was a model for others to follow, including Dani.

"Well, thank you, again." She took her basket, turned, and walked away. What would she do with this many blackberries? She'd be eating them every day for a while, and she popped a warm berry in her mouth as she walked. She wiped her mouth with the back of her hands trying not to drool. The berry tasted better than it looked, and it looked like a picture.

****

Waking early, she traveled back to Corpus Christi the next day. She pulled *Wanderlust* up at the end of the dock where her houseboat had been moored; just in time to see it hoisted from the water. The powerful tugboat was fitted with a hoist and probably used it for just this purpose. Sometimes boats sank in places where they could not be left.

Dani's home hung by a cable as water gushed from all sides and out the screened windows that she'd left open. The door hung open and she could see the corner of the soaked plaid couch that might have been older than her. She wondered what else was sliding around trying to fall out the one and only door.

Tying *Wanderlust* to its mornings, she walked down the dock where she could view the spectacle a little closer. Carla and Ned were watching from their end of the dock. They waved. The arm of the hoist holding the cable swung over the wooden dock and hung there a moment then swung back the opposite way heading to the flatbed trailer on land that would ferry the boat to the dump. It shook from the weight as it swung and something fell from the open door and rolled across the dock, landing against a pier.

And that was it. The boat that had been her home, and her uncle's, was now in a pile on the back of a semitrailer that would take it to its final resting place. The cables were removed, it was strapped in place, and the truck drove away. Dani watched until she could no longer see the truck as it left the dock. Her home was gone. Everything was gone. It felt so final even though she hadn't lived in it for a while. Her life had changed and hopefully changed for the better.

"Well, it's gone," Carla said as they walked up. "I'm sorry, honey. But I hope your new apartment is a good one."

"Yes, it is. And it's probably bigger than the boat was. Anyway, I'm washing dishes at night at Le Chez when I don't have a night tour. I seldom have night tours anyway. So, it's going to work out. It helps pay the rent for the apartment and I won't have to pay rent for the slip here anymore."

"I'm glad things are working out for you. Come down and have a glass of tea with us," Carla said and reached for her arm.

"Thank you. I'd love something to drink. But let me see what dropped out of the houseboat when they lifted it." She nodded toward the pier where she saw the item roll and walked that way.

Lodged up against two piers was the cookie jar that had been hers as a child. She leaned down and picked it up and water drained from the lid that screwed on. It hadn't been that long, but she couldn't remember how much money she had in the jar. A lot had happened over the last few days. Of course it was wet. But money could be dried out.

"This sat in my kitchen," she said as explanation for her actions.

"Well, it's something," Carla said and held out her hand. "How about that tea?"

Back at Carla's boat, Dani sat on the sofa she had used as a bed when her boat first sank. She couldn't remember if she'd ever thanked them for their kindness that night.

"Thank you," she said as she was handed a glass of tea. "And thank you for all you've done for me. I don't know what I'd have done the night the boat sank if it weren't for the two of you."

"Oh, don't mention it. We were glad to help," Carla said. Ned just nodded as usual.

Sun tea. It was so refreshing. It made Dani think she could do the same on her deck at the apartment and have some tea waiting for her when she came in from work. She'd look for a jug next time she shopped.

Carla chatted about fishing and the neighbors on the dock as Dani remained attentive. She tried to act like she was listening but in reality, her mind kept returning to Cody. Where was he and when would she see him again?

Draining her glass, she said her goodbyes and picked up the still leaking cookie jar that she had left outside the door then headed back to her boat.

Back on *Wanderlust*, Dani set the cookie jar on the floor next to the captain's chair and headed back to the island. She might still pick up an afternoon fare before her shift at Le Chez that evening.

When she pulled into the dock, there were no tourists to be found.

She walked back to her apartment and took the cookie jar to the kitchen sink, unscrewing the lid. With the plug in the drain, she leaned the jar on its side. Brown, smelly water splashed out—followed by green money. And it continued to roll out. Dollar bills and bills of larger denomination. When had she last counted this? Impatiently she dumped the entire jar upside down and then pulled all the bills from the jar. It was as full of cash as it was water. She stared at the sight in her sink, then grabbed paper towels and spread them on the countertop. With something to soak up the water she began to lay the bills on the counter. And soon they covered it. Most of them were small denominations, but it was still money.

She stepped back and gazed at the sight and suddenly felt the need to close the blinds. She never had to worry about being robbed since she had nothing. But now, she was nervous. Without thinking, she covered the bills with another layer of paper towels telling herself it was to soak up water, but she knew better. She wanted to hide the money from prying eyes. So, this was what it was like to be rich. And she laughed to herself.

She looked around for something heavy to press the money flat as it dried out but could find nothing but a jelly roll pan from under the oven. It didn't weigh much, but she laid it on top of the most wrinkled pile. If it was crinkled, so be it. Money was money.

Chapter 25

The coffee brewed as she stood in her pajamas and looked at the money on her kitchen counter in the early morning light. It had dried overnight. She crossed her arms and stood there staring. Then she made up her mind. She couldn't worry about being robbed. She had enough to worry about with Cody. And with the way Joey came and went out of her apartment and the fact that it didn't lock, she'd take the money to the bank. It was time to remove one more worry from her list. Maybe it was time to turn her hard-earned cash into a business bank account, not just a cookie jar. She'd only had a personal account up until now, and if she were to be a successful businesswoman, she needed a business account. To succeed in business you had to take some risks. And if her life had taught her anything lately, it was that she had survived plenty of risks.

On the kitchen countertop she stared at the lumps under the paper towels. Running her hands over the top she knew it was time. She gathered the bills into stacks of similar denominations and then tallied them up. She counted a second time and it came out the same. She had over $1000. She had never had that much money in one place at one time, other than the net worth of *Wanderlust* and the houseboat that now made its home at the dump.

She walked to the closet. She put on her nicest outfit, the sundress and sandals from Meg. Then she placed the cash in a bag and walked to the bank. Sandhill Island had not had a bank until recently, but in the last few years it had become apparent that the island needed more than just an ATM. So, a Corpus Christi bank took the bait and opened a branch office on the island with a local islander in charge. It had been a good business decision.

She walked into the artificially cool building and asked to see the loan officer who had helped her buy *Wanderlust*.

"Hi, Dani," he said smiling. "It's good to see you. How are you and what can I do for you today?" He gestured for her to sit.

"I am doing well, thank you, and I have two things," she said sitting down with the bag at her feet. "I think it's time I opened a business account. And I may want to buy a second boat in the future. A tour boat for Cody to pilot. Not right now, but soon."

"Branching out, huh? I can help you with that," he said with a smile. "But first, let's set up that new account."

****

Dani spent the day taking a few people out on tours. Several times she stopped by the apartment and glanced up the stairs. There was nothing on her deck. When did they want her and when would she see her brother again? It had been days, and she hoped he was okay. She'd do whatever she had to do to see him.

Between tourists, Dani trotted to the top of the stairs and opened the door of her unlocked apartment—and almost tripped over it.

The bag she was waiting for was inside her home. She pushed it with her foot and the slip of paper that gave her coordinates and time was underneath again. This time they would meet at dusk. She shoved the paper in her pocket. The product she was to ferry into open water was in her apartment. Did that make her an accessory? Of course she was. She was a drug mule now, whether she liked it or not.

The duffle bag had been placed inside her door. She shivered like it was the dead of winter. They'd been in her home! Of course it didn't lock—but this had to end. She didn't feel safe anymore—because she wasn't.

Chapter 26

Dani looked out to sea from her deck and knew she couldn't put her conversation with Sam off any longer. She had to tell him she wouldn't be coming in tonight and she had to sound nonchalant. She walked in the back door of the restaurant where he was already cooking.

"Hi, Sam," she said trying to smile. "I wanted to let you know, I'll be unable to wash dishes for you tonight. I have…I have a tour to take out later."

He turned and looked her up and down assessing what she just said, or how she said it.

"Of course, that was the deal. The tours come first. You just work when you can." He went back to stirring sauce that smelled like heaven, and she turned to go.

She hated to do that to him when he had been so kind. She'd make this up to him as soon as she got back from her meeting with the drug dealers. But the best thing about going out tonight was she would get to see her brother. And this time she would bring Cody with her, no matter what.

After once again fueling, Dani headed out in the late afternoon sun. Jimmy was on break, so he didn't hassle her about the amount of fuel she bought. No one seemed to see her leave, as far as she knew, but it was a small island, and everyone knew everyone's business. Maybe under the circumstances that wasn't a bad thing, she thought.

****

The man with the floppy hat walked to the door of the police station and propped his broom outside. He wouldn't be needing it indoors.

He was used to being in disguise. He had learned a long time ago how to blend in and he did it well. He could learn the area where he worked, and he instinctively knew just who to talk to and who to avoid. Poppy was the perfect person. He knew everyone and he kept his mouth shut. He didn't even charge for information. He could have, but it had probably never even occurred to the man how valuable he was. The Cleaner was certain that Poppy could use the money, and he'd offered more than once, but Poppy said no. It was just stuff he knew, and he was willing to share.

The Cleaner opened the door to the station and felt the cool air. The small building had two rooms with a receptionist upfront. It was littered with old newspapers and smelled of stale coffee. There was a box of petrified doughnuts on the desk—obviously not freshly baked today. The receptionist was on the phone and held up one finger to let him know to wait.

"Can I help you?" called the voice from the other room. The young man behind the desk stood and walked toward The Cleaner. "Constable Riggs," he said sticking out his hand in greeting. A large black dog lay in the corner and raised its head, sighed, and lay back down. There was nothing to see here.

The Cleaner surveyed the room as he took off his hat and sunglasses. He was younger than he appeared in the hat. His ice blue eyes looked around, then zeroed in on the constable. His military style haircut made him look less like a homeless person. He pulled an ID from his pocket and showed it to the constable. "Special Agent Kent Murphy, DEA. You have a bit of a drug problem on your little island."

Riggs hesitated. "Drug Enforcement Administration? I don't think there is a drug problem on Sandhill Island. You must be mistaken."

"Well, it is just getting started. Drugs are being funneled from Corpus Christi to the island and then into open waters by Dani Brown, on her tour boat. And we believe her brother, Cody Brown, is in on it with her."

The constable shifted uncomfortably. "Now I know you're wrong. I've known Dani Brown for many years and I'm sure she's not delivering drugs with her boat. Cody might be a bit of a problem, but he's seldom around anyway."

Agent Murphy looked unimpressed with this new information. "I'm actually after Joseph Rossi, aka Joey. He's the brains behind the scheme. I think the Browns are just pawns in a bigger game. You know that Ms. Brown's houseboat was recently sunk in Corpus Christi where she lived? I was there the night it happened but unable to apprehend the men who did it. I believe one of them was Rossi. It's possible that they forced Ms. Brown into delivering product for them by sinking her houseboat."

Constable Riggs stared at the man in his office. "That's awful. We all knew about Dani's houseboat but had no idea who did it or why. She took an apartment above Le Chez since she had nowhere to live. But I had no idea about any of the rest of this. You can find Dani at that apartment. I'll take you there if you want to talk to her."

The DEA agent looked around the room and then

back at the constable. "Thank you, but she's gone. She left on her tour boat. She's not tied up at the dock or giving any tours of the island."

"Well, that's unusual. She's normally on that boat seven days a week. She gets as many tourists as possible. She's a hard worker."

"Yes, I've watched her for a while. She doesn't normally leave this late."

Riggs looked out his window then back at the DEA agent. "Tell me about this Rossi. He's from Corpus Christi? He doesn't live on my island."

"I believe he's been here a time or two. But he lives in Corpus. We think he's the middleman. The drugs are coming from a Mexican cartel with money and resources. They have fast boats and are always on the run. Rossi is probably working through them and trying to enlarge his little operation."

"Well, I still don't believe Dani is in on this—unless she was forced, as you said. But tell me what you need the island police force to do. We're available."

"Well first off, I'm undercover. This has to stay within the police force. Do you have any more manpower?"

"Just one, Constable Skaggs. We split the day and night shifts up. Not much goes on around here normally. Just the occasional drunk tourist or something. It's quiet here." He reached for the phone. "I'll call the other constable in, and we can discuss what needs to be done."

The DEA agent sat down on the chair in front of the desk to wait. The dog stood and walked over wagging its tail and nosed the agent. Agent Murphy leaned over and ruffled the dog's ears.

Riggs smiled. "That's Sarge. He's a fixture around

here. In fact, I got him from a local after the last crime here on the island. Like I said, it's pretty quiet around here normally."

Chapter 27

It didn't take long for Dani to find the place where she was to wait for Cody. It seemed she traveled the three miles much faster than last time. She flipped on the running lights on her boat knowing she would need them soon. This was getting to be a habit and she knew it would never stop. They would use her and Cody until they were dead and then move on to the next person.

Staring into the sinking of the afternoon sun, she knew she needed help. The time had come. She had tried to explain to Sam why she wouldn't be at work tonight and she wondered if he believed her. But she had bigger problems than Sam. She had Cody.

Then, she made another decision. Cody was her biggest problem, and he had to come first. And she needed help with this problem. Why did it take her so long to come to this conclusion?

Pulling her phone from her back pocket, she dialed 911 and it went straight to the constable's office on the island. Suddenly she didn't know what to say.

"Constable Riggs," the voice on the other end answered.

She stammered.

"Hello?"

"Um this is Dani Brown and I needed to talk to you about a potential problem…"

"Dani, this is Bill Riggs. We've wondered where

you went. Are you okay?"

"Not really, Bill. It's Cody. He's been kidnapped and I'm trying to get him back from some really bad guys. I'm in open water and waiting on them…"

"Where are you, Dani? We'll come get you."

Dani pulled the paper from her pocket and was about to give him coordinates when the cigar boat raced past. She hadn't even seen him coming this time. She was knocked sideways by the waves and the slip of paper fell from her hand. She grabbed for it, but it was quickly washed overboard.

"Hello, hello?" the voice on the other end called.

The boat pulled back around slowly and once more the dealer jumped onto her boat with the line to tie them together. Hoping he didn't see her; she tossed her cell phone on the bench without clicking off. Maybe they could get a trace on her phone if the line were still open. The phone promptly slid between the cushions and out of sight.

Her brother sat slumped in the back seat of the cigar boat and barely glanced up at her. Tacos or no tacos, Cody looked worse today than last time. She had to get him back home. She should have called the police earlier. How did she think she could manage this herself? Then she realized there was an extra person in the speed boat this time: the one who was on her boat last time, the driver, and the backseat dealer who sat with Cody. The extra man made the quick boat very crowded.

"Hey, lady captain," the dealer who had jumped aboard her vessel said. "I was rude and didn't introduce myself to you last time. My name is Rodriquez. You have something for me?"

"Yes, it's here." She pointed to the bag on the floor

by her feet. "But Cody leaves with me this time."

Dani saw a smile pass across the face of the man who appeared to be in charge just before he pulled his cell phone from his pocket and mumbled something into it. He reached for the bag and unzipped it glancing in. Then he zipped it closed and tossed it into the other boat.

"He'll go back when I say. I still have need of him—and you." He pointed a dirty finger at Dani, and she involuntarily backed up a half step.

Appalled at her reaction, she stepped forward once more. "No, Cody goes with me, or I'll tell the authorities of this deal and where to find you."

He leaned in within touching distance—his hot breath on her face. "Do you not see my boat? She can travel over one hundred miles an hour. By the time you called anyone, we'd be long gone. So, the next time you are needed you will once more bring me the package that will be delivered to you. And maybe, just maybe, your brother will once again dine on tacos tonight." He glanced at Cody. "Or maybe not."

Rodriquez nodded to the dealer on the cigar boat, then quickly glanced back at her. His black eyes stared her down.

"Carlos!" Rodriquez shouted to the man with the mustache on the cigar boat. He stood and tossed a second bag to the man who was in charge. Rodriquez caught it with ease. He held it out to her. "Take this back to the island and deliver it to Joey. Then you wait and you'll receive instructions." He leaned in closer once more to make a point. "Or he'll burn down your precious dock. It will all be your fault. Your neighbors' boats, and maybe your neighbors, will perish and you'll never see your brother again."

Dani saw red. She knocked the bag from the dealer's hand and raced to the bow of *Wanderlust*. "Cody!" she shouted with her hand outstretched ready to pull him onto her boat. Cody made a leap for her but was knocked sideways almost out of the cigar boat.

Dani felt herself grabbed from behind by her shirt and hoisted back. Then Rodriquez raced to the edge to retrieve the still floating bag which sat at an angle slowly filling with water. As he leaned over the edge, she saw an opportunity and shoved him trying to knock him into the water. But he was much larger and stronger than her. He threw her back into the boat and grabbed the soggy bag swinging it around. As he once more lunged at her, the bag caught her in the jaw, knocking her sideways.

She barely remembered hitting the water face first.

Dani's only thought when she hit the water was she had to get back onboard *Wanderlust*. Cody needed her. She could hear him yelling, but barely conscious, she didn't have the strength to call back.

Dani felt the dark water cover her as she descended slowly from the surface. At first, she felt unconcerned as she watched the bubbles rise, and then she realized she was sinking—in the ocean. She couldn't drown this easily. She had lived near the ocean all her life and loved and respected it. Surely it wouldn't kill her. Then she thought of Cody and anger once more surged through her. He was still on the cigar boat, a prisoner of the drug dealers. There was more to this than just her sinking below the surface. If he died, what would she tell Mom? She was told to look after him. He was her baby brother. Slowly she remembered they were no longer children and she and Cody were the only ones left alive in her family. She wouldn't have to explain anything to Mom.

But she still had to survive this and try to get Cody home.

Thoughts ran through her head wondering if maybe she could climb aboard her own boat and overpower the dealer who now planned to pilot it. Even as she thought it, she knew she couldn't take back control of her own boat. What would she do with the man? She couldn't leave him to die in the ocean, and she didn't have the strength to subdue him. The best she could do was hang on and try not to be found out. *Wanderlust* was her savior for now if she could just hold out long enough and not be spotted.

Using her arms, she pushed toward the surface where she could breathe. She began to follow the bubbles when her head banged on metal underneath *Wanderlust's* uneven bottom. She felt along the bottom until she found a place to surface. An air pocket. She could breathe. She heard the noise of men arguing in Spanish and she remained still. Her head was above water even though she was under the hull of *Wanderlust*. Slowly, using her hands, she moved from under the boat to the side. She could hang on until the drug dealers left. Or maybe she could still get Cody from their boat to hers. Of course, even if she did, there was no way *Wanderlust* could outrun the cigar boat, but it was worth a try to hold on. She had little choice.

She worked her way around the edge of the tour boat to the bow and peeked at the man who leaned over and looked into the water. Was he looking for her? She slipped back where she could not be seen and held the edge of the tour boat waiting to see what would happen next. Then she heard Rodriquez call to another member of his group.

On board, orders were barked and someone started

the engine of her boat. She heard the speedboat race away leaving only her tour boat with someone else at the helm. They were going to leave her in the middle of the ocean if she didn't do something quickly. Just as the tour boat began to move, she was slapped in the face with a tiny life jacket that hung from the side. She had left it to dry in the afternoon sun after a tour. Its straps dangled down low enough she could catch them and she hung on for dear life hoping no one saw her. How long she could hang on the side of the tour boat was anyone's guess. But she would try.

****

Rodriquez searched the water where Dani fell. There were no signs she was alive. He stood and rubbed his head to think what to do. He didn't need a dead woman in this deal.

"Carlos!" Rodriquez yelled again at the man still on the cigar boat. "She's gone. Take the tour boat to Mustang Island; you know where I mean. He'll give you a good price for it. When you are done, meet us back in Corpus."

"Right, boss," Carlos said as he leapt easily from the cigar boat to the tour boat. The men traded places and then untied the vessels.

Rodriquez shouted orders to the man remaining on the speed boat and the boat roared to life.

"Dani!" Cody screamed as he scanned the dark water searching for his sister. He was shoved into his seat just before the cigar boat raced away.

****

In the quiet dark after the cigar boat departed, Carlos was left to pilot the tour boat to Mustang Island. He had told his wife he'd be home tonight. She'd be worried.

But she knew he had a job to do, and she was wasting their time worrying. It accomplished nothing. He'd be there when he got there. But he was missing another ball game. His son wasn't happy last time. The boy knew his dad's job took a lot of time, but he really wanted to show his dad his skills. He was good—maybe major league good someday. But Carlos had a job to do and if he played his cards right, he'd see the next game. He'd hurry as much as he could.

Having lived in the area his whole life, Carlos knew how to find most of the islands that dotted the seashore in this area of the Gulf. He started the engine of the tour boat and turned in the direction of Mustang Island. The woman had a nice boat. It seemed to be well maintained and the engine was smooth. He'd like a boat like this someday. Maybe he could make a living ferrying tourists around. Then he wouldn't have to take orders from all the Rodriquez's in the world. Maybe he should just keep on going past Mustang Island and begin a new life. Or maybe not. He knew Rodriquez would find him and it wouldn't be good if he did.

Carlos checked the fuel gauge and wondered if the boat could travel that far on half a tank, but he had a job to do and he knew better than to fail where Rodriguez was concerned. He pushed the tour boat closer into shore. He wanted to be able to see the lights of the coast, and he didn't want to get lost. If he could see the lights along the shore, he knew he was going in the direction of Mustang Island. Three miles out it was easy to get disoriented, especially after dark.

Chapter 28

The cigar boat sped away knocking Cody into the empty seat. He shouted for Dani but his voice was cut off by the wind and the noise of the engine. Was she okay? He thought he saw her head bob up after she was knocked overboard. If anyone could survive out here it was Dani, but she was miles from shore. No one could swim that far.

These thoughts ran through his head as the speedboat raced across the water. Soon *Wanderlust* was lost to sight in a sea of waves. He settled back into his seat wondering how long he could keep this up. He was sick, hungry, thirsty, needed a hit, and his siter was probably drowned. He knew he would be next.

The cigar boat flew across the water, its hull sometimes leaving the surface of the water and racing across air from wave to wave. At another time, Cody would have been impressed with the speed and performance of the vessel. But not today. Who knew where it was going and where he would end up. But he stared out at the never-ending water and wished he were alone on the ocean. He'd drive the boat to parts unknown and never come back.

Then he heard sputtering and the cigar boat slowed. Maybe the boat wasn't as magnificent as it appeared.

The dealers were yelling at each other and smoke was rising from the engine choking Cody. He tried to climb into the front seat to get away from the smoke but was thrown back into the corner. The engine quickly ground to a halt.

"Move over, junkie," the smuggler said as he climbed in the back seat and raised the engine housing.

Cody scooted over as far as the narrow seat would allow and watched as the man stood and stared into the engine compartment. It was obvious he knew nothing about engines. He yelled in Spanish at what was left of his crew. Cody didn't understand what he said but the other dealers' services were needed.

Cody was then roughly shoved to the front as the second dealer took his place and they looked into the cavernous engine compartment. Most of the smoke had blown away and now just a small plume wafted out slowly. Cody began to smell fuel and knew that wasn't a good thing for any engine.

"Junkie, get back here," Rodriquez said. "You know anything about engines? Your sister has a boat. Fix this."

"I don't know anything about engines and why would I help you anyway?" As soon as the words left his mouth, Cody knew it was the wrong thing to say.

He was roughly grabbed by the shirt and dragged to the back where there was not enough room for three.

More arguments Cody could not understand finally ended with the second dealer shoved up front once more. Rodriquez pushed Cody's face toward the engine for a closer look. "Fix it or you die," he said and began punching buttons on his phone probably calling for help as he stepped to the front of the boat once more.

The front-seat dealer was already on his phone desperately begging for assistance. A sudden wave rolled something against Cody's bare foot. A flare. And it was just within reach. He could set it off and call for help. Not that anyone would be around to see it. Then his foot began to feel cool. Looking down, he realized the fuel he smelled earlier was now pooling in the bottom of the boat. Cody knew what was wrong with the engine—it wasn't getting fuel. Not if the bottom of the boat was filling up with it.

And the fuel could be ignited by the flare if he could keep it dry.

Of course they'd all die, but didn't they deserve to? Him included? His sister was probably drowned by now. She couldn't tread water forever. He didn't want to spend what was left of his life on this boat with two morons who threatened to kill him anyway. So, why not?

"What is it? What is wrong with my boat?" the dealer screamed from the front of the boat. "Did you not hear me say you would die if you didn't fix it?"

Yes, Cody knew he was about to die.

"I heard you. And I know what is wrong with your boat," he said as he looked the dealer in the eye for probably the first time since the whole smuggling incident started. He realized he hadn't looked anyone in the eye for a long time. What had happened to his confidence? Had it been eaten up like his brain by the stuff he injected and snorted? That's when he made a decision that would change what was left of his life.

"Your engine isn't getting fuel."

The dealer turned to scream at his partner when Cody popped the top off the flare. The string fusèe fell out and he glanced back at the men in the front of the boat for a half second. He had only one chance. Aiming at the bottom of the boat, he dove overboard and at the same time pulled the strings downwards igniting the fuel in the bottom of the boat.

The explosion was instantaneous.

Cody felt the blast as it threw him far from the boat and he landed deep in the water. He couldn't breathe but the water probably saved him from being burned to death or blown to bits. At first, he couldn't decide which was up and which was down. Then he remembered the bubbles. Follow the bubbles, Dani always told him. They will take you to the surface—where there was oxygen.

He remembered very little about the blast. But he remembered surfacing finally. Saltwater makes a body buoyant—another lesson from Dani—and she was right. He was lying on his back and breathing and that was everything. His ears rang and he might never hear again and the skin on his face, neck, and hands burned like fire in the salty water. He felt the bandage that had covered his neck flopping in the waves, and he thought of blood in the water. Sharks were attracted to blood. But the wound had begun to heal in the last few days. Then why did it burn like fire in the salt water. He must be bleeding again from his neck and maybe his face and hands. He didn't need to attract any predators. Sharks were the last thing he needed tonight. Those things terrified him. Having lived next to the ocean all his life, he had never gotten used to them. He knew they were out there, and he knew they were continuous eating machines. He didn't want to become someone's dinner.

He stared into the night sky barely conscious but breathing. He was in the middle of the ocean without a boat or any means of flotation. He finally had that night alone on the ocean he'd dreamed about.

He knew he was about three miles from the beach if they traveled parallel to land. He was unsure which way the cigar boat traveled. But it didn't head into shore, he was sure of that. Three miles from land in the dark sea was the same as being in the middle of the ocean. He was a land animal and land animals needed to stay on land. At the moment, he was the opposite of a fish out of water.

Slowly, it occurred to him that if he was alive, he might not be the only one and he looked in the direction he thought the boat had been—but saw nothing. Rodriquez was probably dead. And he might soon join him. There were currents that might carry the debris away and he had no idea how long he had been floating there semi-conscious. He didn't know where the speedboat was or if there was enough of it left to even find. He turned in a slow circle wondering which direction was home but had no idea. Yes, there were currents, and where they would take him was the question. He lay back and looked at the stars just breathing—thankful to be alive. He'd float as long as he could. Daylight would come and maybe a boat would find him. Maybe he could survive if he stayed calm. It had been days since he had had a fix and the dts were sure to kick in any time now. Dts, or Delirium tremens, would not kill him, only make him wish he were dead. He was cold, hungry, and needed a fix. The deep blue ocean wasn't his only problem. He had to keep his head on straight. He wished his sister were here to help him. Dani had a way about her that kept people calm. But he wouldn't wish his situation on her or anyone else. Then it occurred to him she might be in this same situation—and he laughed aloud. If she was lucky, she was in this same situation, or she might be dead.

When something large bumped him from underneath.

Chapter 29

Dani clung to the life jacket that hung on the side of *Wanderlust* for what seemed like hours. She knew it hadn't been hours, but her arms ached. Soon they would burn and then she'd want to scream. But they'd have to pry her fingers loose before she'd let go. She had no idea where the man who had hijacked her boat was heading. But as long as she could hang on, she was going wherever he was going.

In the length of time since the dealers took over her boat the sun had set and now it was dark. She looked behind her and then twisted around to see in front. She could see no lights of any sort. She had been three miles out from Sandhill Island when she met the dealers, and she knew it wouldn't take hours to get back. So where were they going?

The full moon was covered now and then by clouds and soon the wind kicked up making the water choppy. She continued to look for lights in the distance. She didn't know how long they'd been traveling but she knew her craft and it wouldn't run forever on the partial tank of fuel.

Then a pinpoint of light caught her eye—then covered up. Then she saw it again. A star? It was hard to decide from the angle where she hung what was sky and what was water. Then it appeared again, and soon more tiny points of brightness appeared, too. It had to be the island.

That thought made her relax enough her arms almost quit screaming. She laid her head on her arm and said a little prayer for her own survival but also her brother's. Wherever he was. She was still a long way from home, and she couldn't quit now. Slowly, she began to understand they were not headed toward the island. He was traveling past it. He couldn't go back to Sandhill Island. Everyone knew *Wanderlust* there. He had to go somewhere else. She looked around once more. The direction he was going was probably Mustang Island. And he didn't have enough fuel for that. He'd have to stop somewhere, or he'd run out of fuel in the middle of the night miles from shore. Then what would he do? Would he find her hanging on the side of the boat? She couldn't allow that.

She decided then; she wasn't going to Mustang Island with him. Who knew what would happen when she was discovered hitching a ride with a drug dealer. And it was a long swim to Sandhill Island even if she could see the lights. But without the boat, she would be left stranded in the night miles from shore.

Could she swim to the island from where she was now? No. Her arms were tired just from hanging on to the life jacket. She had to have a plan.

Her hand slipped from the wet life jacket she had begun to think of as her savior, and she let it hang for a minute and relax then traded and hung on with the slightly rested arm. The strap from the jacket hung in her face and she felt it as it brushed across her nose.

Maybe that was it. She could use the life jacket and kick her way toward the lights on Sandhill Island. It was better than the idea of swimming.

She looked up and pulled on the child-sized life jacket she clung to. It held fast, which had been to her advantage until now. There was an adult sized one, too. Maybe it would be better. Stretching, she tried to reach it without letting go of the tiny one, but she couldn't bridge the distance. Readjusting, she reached again, but without success. She'd have to get the smaller one loose and use it. It was better than nothing.

Concentrating on the child-sized life jacket which had taken care of her so far, she yanked again at the clip that held the jacket to the lines running along the side of the boat. She used that line to dry the life jackets daily after the customers finished their tours. Thankfully, she had left them there to dry or she would have nothing to hold on to now. Why had she secured them so well?

"Let go!" she said louder than she meant to.

Carlos twisted and looked all around him. She hunched down with her hand over her mouth. What was she thinking? She once more grabbed the life jacket with both hands.

Carlos searched the dark night and then shrugged and once more began to pilot the boat.

A wave hit her in the face again slamming her into the side of the boat and this time leaving her hanging on by one hand. She couldn't lose the grip she had on the flotation device. The waves were beginning to pick up. She didn't need a rough sea at a time like this, but maybe they would push her toward Sandhill Island. One way or another, she needed to let go of her precious boat and take her chances.

She reached up once more grabbing the life jacket with both hands. She put one foot up on the side of the boat and yanked with all her might. The clip held fast.

Another wave and the boat rocked first one way and then the next. And suddenly the clip let go sending her splashing backwards. A wave caught her in the face, and she swallowed salt water. When she surfaced, she no longer held on to the child sized flotation device that was to be her savior. She had lost contact with it when the wave pushed her under. And *Wanderlust* was pulling away without her. She spun around looking for the life jacket as the boat left her behind. She tried to swim and catch up with it, but it was too fast.

She was floating unsupported in the ocean as her boat pulled away. Why was she so stupid to let it go? She needed it. Now she was on her own to swim to the island. There were waves and currents that would help. But what if they weren't going the right way? She stared once more at the tiny pinpoints of light. She had to try to swim toward the island. Taking a deep breath, she slowly stroked, keeping her arms underwater so not to tire them anymore than they already were.

She would not drown, she told herself. She had to stay alive.

Her already fatigued arms were quickly becoming useless. She rolled over on her back and kicked her feet. Now and then, she'd stop to make sure she was headed in the right direction then begin to kick again.

When something smacked her in the head, she instinctively grabbed the strap from the small jacket.

It was like a gift from heaven.

It was too small to put on, but she could use it to support her exhausted arms as she kicked her feet. Another wave washed over her, and she looked once more in the distance. It seemed the bright lights were getting brighter, especially in one place. Was that the dock? It didn't matter. She knew she was headed in the right direction, and she kicked with renewed vigor—for a while. Soon she realized she hadn't eaten all day, and she had been in the water for hours. She was becoming exhausted. First her arms and now her legs. How long could she hold out?

Chapter 30

Jimmy knew it was time to leave. Something was up on the island, Joey had offered him a job in Corpus, and Marybeth was beginning to act flaky. She hardly ever met him after the taco stand closed. She was always busy. He even wondered if she was really pregnant. He hadn't been to the doctor with her. In fact, had she been to the doctor or just read one of those pregnancy tests you get at the grocery store?

Then he saw her with that guy from Mustang Island that worked as a cabana-boy. At least he had been told that was where the dude was from when he asked around. He watched the two of them from behind a fuel tank as she laughed and flipped her hair. It was obvious she was stepping out on him. And as soon as the guy walked away and Marybeth was alone, Jimmy left his post and walked her way. It was time to confront her.

"Marybeth," he said and waved. He wasn't supposed to be working that day and Marybeth seemed surprised to see him.

She waved back tentatively and glanced in the direction cabana-boy walked.

"Jimmy," she said hesitantly.

"Who's the guy and why aren't you home with your mom?" He got right to the point.

"Jimmy, I thought this was your day off."

"Obviously, or you wouldn't be here. So, who is he

and what are you doing with him?" He glanced at her stomach and thought for the hundredth time, she still wasn't showing.

"That's Todd. He's from Mustang Island."

"Were you going to tell me about him or just let me guess? You said I was the only one, but you must have lied about that too. You're not really pregnant, are you?"

"I...I thought I was and then, well you know. Maybe I lost it. I don't know."

"Yeah, I'll bet. That is the oldest story in the book. You going to lie to him about being pregnant, too? Is it your way out of this life to hook some guy into marrying you?" He rubbed a hand over his face. "I understand about wanting to get away from here, but maybe lying isn't the way."

"I didn't lie; I thought I was pregnant!"

"And then along comes cabana-boy." Jimmy looked out to sea, and then back at his place on the dock. A boat was coming in probably for fuel. "I gotta go. Have a good life," he said as he walked away. How could she do this to him? Maybe it was for the best. He was pissed and at the same time relieved. He didn't want to be a husband and father, at least not now.

He walked back to the dock with his head down and never looked back. Marybeth was in his past and on top of that he was free. Somehow, he still didn't feel good about it.

"Fill her up, sir?" he asked as he got back to his post. No, this was not going to be his life.

And he decided, when he got his dinner break, he'd pack what little he planned to take with him, all of what was left of his money, and catch the last ferry off the island tonight. He had the address of Joey's apartment, and he would just wait until Joey got back. He'd just not show back up at the job. They'd understand eventually. He'd leave Mom and Dad a short note, not giving them any details or they'd come looking for him, and then Sandhill Island would be in his rearview mirror. Maybe working for Joey someday he could afford a real rearview mirror, attached to a car, that took him where he wanted to go.

It was the best chance he'd been offered so far, and he could work for Joey. He seemed like a generous guy and Jimmy was a hard worker. He'd prove himself.

It was time to go.

****

The more Shayla thought about it the more she didn't like the guy Poppy called The Cleaner. And she was concerned about Cody. It was late, but maybe she should talk to the local police and see if they had any way to search for him. Evidently The Cleaner was looking for him, too, and that might not be good.

She had finished her last art project on the island and was about to go visit her mom on the mainland but decided on a detour before heading home. Bill Riggs was the constable on the island, and she'd known him all her life. She pulled into the parking lot of the tiny building that held what law enforcement they had on the island.

As she reached for the doorknob, it opened and the constables both walked out together. Surprised, she stepped back. "Bill, are you in a hurry?"

"Just heading out, Shayla. What can I do for you?" He walked toward the cruiser parked beside the building.

"Have you heard from Cody Brown lately? I mean, I talked to Dani and he's using again. I assumed he was, but she confirmed it. And you know that can't be good.

And then there was this guy talking to Poppy about Cody. I don't know his name, but Poppy called him…"

Agent Murphy stepped from the shadows and joined the group. He glanced at Shayla and then sauntered to the backdoor of the car.

Shayla's mouth dropped open.

"He's with us," Riggs said. "I'll keep an eye out for Cody. Don't worry about him. He and Dani will be fine." He patted her on the shoulder and all three men climbed into the police cruiser and headed toward the dock. Shayla stood looking after them with a million questions.

****

Hours before, Joey received the call from Rodriquez, his cartel contact. If Dani wasn't back with his money before midnight, he was to set the dock on fire as promised. It was a threat that could be dangerous, and he hoped he wouldn't have to fulfill this job. He'd have to get in and out without being seen. It could be tricky. Most of the fishermen and tours were docked before dark, but people hung around. He filled the two hand-held gasoline cans and placed them carefully in the trunk of his car. He had to get to the island before the last ferry and then lay low until everyone was gone from the dock area. Then, after the deed was done, he had to hide until he could get back to the mainland early in the morning on the first ferry. It was a dangerous mission, but he had to keep Rodriquez happy.

By 11:00 when Dani hadn't shown up, he tried to call Rodriquez, but he didn't get an answer. Maybe he was out too far in that sleek boat and didn't have a signal. But something didn't feel right. He waited in his car parked next to the dock for a while and wondered when he should do the deed. Every time he almost got out of his car someone showed back up. According to Jimmy at the dock, there was a guy who lived on his boat but he was tied up at the other side so Joey shouldn't run into him. Then there was Poppy. He normally left before dark. But Joey hadn't seen him.

It might be that Jimmy could come in handy. He needed someone who was sharp. Joey wondered if Jimmy would consider moving to Corpus when this was over. He'd try him out. He'd already told the kid to meet him at his apartment, and he thought the boy would show up.

Sitting in the car with the windows open, he sprayed himself with insect repellant to keep the mosquitoes at bay. It almost worked. He hated the water, boats, and most of all, mosquitoes. Why he lived in this environment, he had no idea. Except this was where his business was. If he could enlarge his business and get it off the ground, he'd move north and let the underlings do the dirty work on the coast. He could expand his trade to the people who didn't live next to fishy-smelling water and all those mosquitoes. He batted at another one crushing it on his leg. It left a bloody spot, and he wondered whose blood was now soaking into his pant leg—his own or someone else's? Those bloodsuckers carried disease!

He stared at the long dock. It didn't used to be this long before it was rebuilt after being destroyed in a hurricane. Why they built it this long, he had no idea, but it might have something to do with growing the economy. Business, he understood. He was a businessman. But not all the slips were filled, which meant rent was going uncollected. They should hire him to fill those empty slots.

No, he wanted nothing to do with being that close to the water.

He knew one thing. He wasn't going to set the fuel tanks at the end of the dock on fire. The fuel station that many boats used was off limits. If the fire got that far, he'd be long gone. He had planned to pour his gasoline starting in the middle and then follow the dock both ways. But not near the fuel pumps. That was dangerous and he might not make it out in time. Then he decided to start several yards from the fuel tanks and leave a trail to the land end of the dock. That might be safer. He needed time to get away once the flame was lit. Fire scared him more than water. There was no way he'd be on that dock when it caught fire, business deal or no business deal.

Just as he was about to step out of the car, along came another straggler. This one had a fishing pole over one shoulder and a tackle box in his hand. There was a short stringer of fish in the other hand. Supper, he thought and shuddered. Eating fish was almost as bad as being in the water with them.

The man stopped to tie his shoelace and bat some mosquitoes from around his head. Then he looked off in the distance at the night sky. What was he doing? Joey pulled his hat down over his eyes and slid down into the seat. Within minutes he was snoring. The dock could wait.

Chapter 31

The police cruiser pulled up at the dock on the commercial side. Most of the boats were tied up here. The other side had a few stragglers, but the tourists came to this side to do their business. The tour boats were tied up here and the fuel tanks were at the end of the dock.

The three law enforcement officers climbed out of the cruiser and walked toward the dock in the dark. It was mostly deserted.

They'd been to Dani's apartment and stumbled upon it unlocked. That wasn't too unusual on Sandhill Island. This wasn't the big city. They looked around and found nothing to be concerned about. Riggs knew Dani had only been renting the place a few days and didn't own much since her houseboat had been destroyed. There was no evidence that Cody had been there. The bed was unmade and there were a few groceries in the fridge. The bathroom showed someone had showered, but that was all. Dani wasn't there.

There was no way to look for Cody unless it was at his sister's. Cody was a drifter. If not for his sister, he might never have come to Sandhill Island. But Riggs knew family could draw you in now and then. Even for low lifes like Cody. Riggs was certain he shouldn't judge. He'd never gotten into drugs himself, and he knew they changed people. But Cody had never had any ambition—unlike his sister. If he was here on the island, he was up to no good.

****

Special Agent Kent Murphy, DEA, aka The Cleaner, left his broom in the vehicle. It was a prop, and he didn't need it anymore. His time undercover had come to an end. But it would be better if he weren't recognized. He stood and took off the floppy hat and unbuttoned the long-sleeved shirt revealing a tee shirt and side arm underneath. He tossed the hat and shirt back in the car. Now he knew he looked different. Maybe not official, but different. He surveyed the dock. It was a small town that survived on hard work and long hours. It was a tourist town, for families, and would remain that way if he had anything to say about it. He had no use for drug dealers.

Riggs walked the dock and Murphy followed. "She moors her boat over there. We have to find her. That call sounded serious, and something happened or she wouldn't have just dropped the phone like that. I wish we'd known about this earlier. I guess she didn't trust us to help her out. People get scared and think they have to take care of things themselves, I guess."

Murphy turned to the two constables who normally kept the peace on the island. "So, the tour boat that Ms. Brown pilots normally ties up here, huh?"

Riggs nodded and they looked up and down the lighted dock.

Riggs walked toward the empty slip with the sign *Island Tours by Capt. Dani Brown*. Murphy and Skaggs followed, then Murphy pulled a pen light from his pocket and shone the small flashlight around the empty slip. He watched as the waves jostled the bumpers that hung from the pier. He saw no signs of foul play.

Agent Murphy glanced up as a lone figure walked off the sand toward the dock and waved.

Sam, the chef and owner of Le Chez, walked down the dock and stopped where the men had gathered. "Constables." He stuck out his hand and nodded toward Murphy. "I'm Sam," he said to the agent who didn't respond. "Are you looking for Dani? She didn't work for me tonight. And I was wondering about her, too. She's not in her apartment and *Wanderlust* is gone."

Constable Riggs nodded. "Yeah, we just came from her apartment and were checking where she docks. Do you know what she was doing tonight that kept her from working at the restaurant?"

"No, she was vague saying something about having a late tour. She didn't say where or when. She seemed distracted. I thought she really liked working at Le Chez and then I wondered after she said she wasn't coming in. Poppy said the boat had been tied up all day and he never saw her go out until late this afternoon."

Riggs nodded to Skaggs, who normally worked evenings. "Call Jimmy and ask if she fueled up and when. And see if she got an excessive amount of fuel before she headed out. Let me know what you find out. Murphy and I will take the patrol boat out and look around. You go back to the office and begin to make some phone calls. Surely someone saw Dani."

Riggs turned to the chef. "Sam, thanks for your help and let me know if you hear from Dani."

Sam nodded and headed back to his restaurant.

Murphy followed as Riggs headed to the other side of the dock where they moored the police boat.

"Dani called and was about to give us coordinates when something happened. Let's just hope she still has her cell with her and turned on. We should be able to follow it."

Riggs climbed in the boat as Agent Murphy tossed off the lines that held it and jumped in. Riggs started the engine and backed out of the slip then headed out away from the dock. He thumbed through his cell phone for the app that allowed him to ping Dani's phone, and it didn't take long to find the phone was still on and working. He turned the patrol boat in the direction of her phone. Mustang Island. That must be where she went, at least according to the app.

The weather had begun to turn, and the wind had picked up. The water was becoming choppy, but the police patrol boat took the waves with ease. Riggs glanced at Murphy, and he seemed to be at home on the boat. It wasn't his first time out to sea. Good. With all that was going on tonight Riggs didn't need a novice. Police work was police work unless it took place on the ocean. Then things changed. He handed his cell phone to the DEA agent as he piloted the boat. Nothing was said. Both men knew what they were looking for. So far, there were no lights out on the ocean nearby. Riggs pointed the boat out to deeper water. There were always large ships and shrimpers out, but none seemed to be close to the shore. He thought Dani would keep her boat close to shore if she could, so he turned the boat and headed the other way.

"There's nothing out here but shrimpers. I think she's headed to Mustang Island; it is the closest port besides Sandhill. Let me know if you see anything showing where that phone is. And help me keep an eye out for lights. Surely, she is using her running lights."

Murphy nodded as he scanned the dark water.

****

Carlos pushed the throttle forward on *Wanderlust* and marveled at how smoothly it took the waves. This was a nice boat. It was a shame the lady lost it—and maybe her life. He looked for her and didn't see any signs she came back up. No one could survive out there without something to float on and even then, there were things in the water that were always hungry. He didn't get in that water without a boat. He had no intention of becoming something's lunch. But he couldn't think about the woman now. He had to do as he was told, or he'd end up in the same situation as her. Rodriquez took no prisoners—for long. Cody was just about dead anyway, but without his sister, Cody was outliving his usefulness. Rodriquez would put a bullet in him soon. Or have one of his flunkies do it. Carlos hoped he wasn't around for that.

The clouds parted and the moon shone down enough he could read the instruments. Surely there was a flashlight around here somewhere, he thought, but he did see that the fuel tank was half empty. That was not good. He couldn't push the engine and run out of gas. He throttled back and skimmed along the surface with the full moon shining down. It was a beautiful evening all in all, and he thought of home and a girl he once knew who loved the water. It was a long ride to Mustang Island, and he had nothing else to do.

Carlos kept *Wanderlust* at mid throttle. He was afraid the boat wouldn't make it all the way to Mustang Island and the buyer Rodriquez wanted him to see. In the middle of the night there were very few vessels around and being rescued was not likely. The currents would carry him along and maybe past Mustang Island and he'd have no way to navigate back into port. He even thought about cutting the engine and drifting until he saw the island, then he could restart the engines and pull into port. But he was uncertain which way the currents would take him. It would save fuel. But it might not work. One thing he knew for sure, this tour boat wasn't meant for long trips, which was why Dani kept it close to shore most of the time.

If it hadn't been for the moon and the running lights on the boat, Carlos would not have been able to determine where the water stopped, and the sky began. It was truly spooky when the clouds covered up the moonlight. He'd lived around the ocean all his life and had great respect for the power it wielded.

The first lurch of the engine he attributed to the choppy water. The wind had come up and it was stirring up waves. It had been a while since he parted ways with Rodriquez and headed out and now the fuel gauge read close to empty. Then the engine coughed twice and ground to a halt. Carlos knew there was no restarting it, though he tried countless times before throwing up his hands in defeat.

The running lights would only hold out so long on the battery without the engine running. Then he would be in complete darkness with only the moon. That would make it even more doubtful he'd be found drifting along and rescued. He hoped some good Samaritan came along before Rodriquez found out. Even if someone rescued him, he'd have to face the wrath of Rodriquez. If someone pulled him to shore, he'd run as soon as he hit land and never look back.

****

The police traveled mostly in silence looking deep

into the dark night. Lights were limited in the area close to shore. She had to be out here somewhere. The app was pinging the signal and at least the phone was close by. It had to be sitting on a boat or in her pocket—something that was above water. If the phone ended up in the water, that would be the end of the signal. There was still hope.

And then they saw something up ahead. It had the right configuration of lights and might be Dani's boat. If so, it wasn't moving and seemed to be dead in the water. Maybe they had found her. The ping said they had the right place.

Riggs pulled alongside the boat that he was certain belonged to Dani though he couldn't read the name on the side. A man sat in the captain's chair and Dani was nowhere to be seen.

"Boy, am I glad to see you," Carlos shouted. "She's out of fuel. I should have known better than to get out here without any extra."

Murphy deftly jumped on to the tour boat and walked to where the man stood as Riggs tied the two boats together. "Out of fuel, huh?" Murphy said. "Well, maybe you shouldn't be out on the ocean in this vessel at night. It's a good thing we came along. You have some identification, sir?"

The man smiled and felt his pockets. "No, sir. I guess I left that at home. Who knew how this evening would turn out?"

"Constable," Murphy said. "Does this look like the boat that belongs to Dani Brown? What's the name, *Wanderlust*?"

"Yep, *Wanderlust*, that's the name." Riggs stepped onto the boat and walked to the other side, leaning over. "Says *Wanderlust* right here." He eyed the man who sat on the captain's chair. "Have you seen Ms. Brown tonight?"

Carlos looked over the side of the boat. "I don't know any Ms. Brown. I borrowed this boat from a buddy. I was just going to go to Mustang Island for the night."

Agent Murphy turned to the man on the boat. "A buddy, huh? Did that buddy have a name?"

The man said nothing.

"Well, since this craft is from Sandhill Island and belongs to a friend of ours, we're going to have to take you into custody. We have reason to believe this boat is stolen. Any ideas where Dani Brown, captain of this vessel, is at this time? She should be on her boat."

"Oh no, sir, like I said, I don't know Ms. Brown and I just ran out of fuel."

Riggs began to search the boat for the phone since Dani wasn't there. The app that pinged the phone said she was here—or the phone was. He looked under the seats and then tossed the cushions. And then he saw it. The phone had slipped between two cushions where the customers sat when on tour.

He had her phone. Now where was Dani?

Riggs looked out into the night. "For your sake, she'd better be on the other boat that she met tonight. She called us just before she met with the other boat. We know she was trying to rescue her brother. You haven't seen Cody Brown, have you?"

Carlos had nothing more to say. He didn't resist as Murphy turned him around and placed his hands behind his back handcuffing him. Then they led him to the patrol boat where they made sure he climbed in, and they sat him in the back. Once he was secure, they tied the bow of *Wanderlust* to the stern of the patrol boat and towed it back toward Sandhill Island. Their prisoner was silent as they traveled back home.

Chapter 32

Terrified of what had just hit him, Cody pulled his legs up and looked around. The clouds had come in and were covering the moon making the water even darker. Then he thought he saw a fin in the distance, and it was heading in his direction. Adrenaline ran through him so fast it made his extremities hurt. The last thing he needed tonight was a shark. He'd survived the blast and now this.

A string of hair slid into his eyes, and he shoved it back with one blistered hand that stung like it was on fire. That was when he realized most of his hair was gone. His scalp was blistered and oozed as he rubbed over it. He had been so concerned about surviving the inevitable drowning, he didn't realize he was burned. He also realized his face stung. He held up his hand to see it in the dark, but his vision was worthless. It was probably best he couldn't see it. Burns were the least of his worries tonight.

Then once more he was shoved, this time from behind. Instinctively he screamed even though no one could hear. The shark was back! No, sharks didn't shove. They bit! Or actually they tore at their food—and this one didn't use teeth.

He turned in a circle searching for the fish that would end his life. Then he heard the squeaks and whistles of the dolphin. It rose up in the water in front of him and splashed back down, then once more circled behind him, shoving him forward.

This was not possible.

He'd heard stories of dolphins saving drowning swimmers. But that was on TV. His arms stretched out treading water to keep his head up; the dolphin easily slid under one outstretched arm and passed under it—circled and did it again. It wanted him to grab hold. It was trying to help him.

The clouds parted and the full moon shone once more. The dolphin raised its head and smiled. That was when Cody saw that it had a jagged scar on the top of its head. Scar! How did he find him? How was it possible for the dolphin he and Dani fed at the dock to find him in open water, unless Cody was closer to the island than he thought. Scar often followed Dani's boat out into the ocean. But normally not this far. Maybe there was hope yet. The next time the dolphin slid under Cody's arm he grabbed the fin and clung for dear life. His burned hands cracked as he constricted them to hold on, but it was a good pain. The muscular tail flipper pulled him along and Cody tried to keep his legs out of the way. He knew he would be bruised in the morning from being kicked by the massive tail. Assuming he lived to see morning. He just had to hang on and keep his head above water. The dolphin pulled him along making good time through the dark water. He seemed to know where he was going.

That was when he realized it might be possible that he would see the light of another day. And if he did get out of this alive, things would be different. He would get off the stuff and be kinder to his sister. Maybe just kinder in general. He'd make this up to Dani. She'd tried to do so much for him.

He began to shake—growing weaker. Burns and hunger weren't his only problem. He needed a fix, and he wasn't as young and strong as he used to be. It had been a long time since the tacos last night and even longer since he'd had a hit. He was hungry, exhausted, blistered, and going through withdrawals—in the middle of the ocean. He had no idea how long he could hang on to the dolphin who came to help him. It hadn't occurred to him until now how much strength it took just to hold on.

****

Dani lay in the water with her head on the life jacket wondering when it would become waterlogged and begin to sink. The waves sloshed over her and moved her forward—to where she had no idea. But she knew one thing. Her arms had become useless. They had held her up for about as long as they could even with the help of the flotation device. But without it, she knew she'd be dead by now.

She dozed in and out of consciousness as she floated with her head and arms on the PFD. A personal floatation device was the name it had been given, and somehow, she found that humorous now. Personally, she was floating. And without it, she might not be. So, it was aptly named. Why that made her laugh out loud, she didn't know.

She remembered her mom and uncle made both Dani and Cody wear them as they played in the water off the dock where the houseboat was moored. She and her brother would hang them up as soon as they got out of sight and then splash them with water to keep them wet so the adults would think they wore them. But you couldn't dive to the bottom of the sea in a life jacket. And the bottom, where there was sand and debris, was where the fun was. They had snorkels and goggles and could see things from the surface that caught their attention. They had to go down and investigate. Consequently, they became strong swimmers, and both developed a love of the water and all the creatures that lived there. They loved to play with the crabs and small fish since the bigger and more dangerous ones never came that close to shore.

One day Dani cut her arm on a metal band that hung on the underneath side of the dock. She accidentally kicked Cody as she swam to the surface, and he came up behind her.

"What are you doing? That hurt!" he shouted.

She held her arm out for him to see.

"Oh crap!" he shouted. "Get out of the water before the sharks smell blood!"

"Cody, I don't think sharks come in this shallow," she said as she held her arm and kicked to the side.

"What are you kids doing and where are your life jackets?" Dani looked up to see her mother and uncle staring down at them in the water. Their life jackets hung on the dock.

"It's my fault, Mom," Cody called. "I wanted to show Dani something and she got cut. It's my fault."

It wasn't, but as children he always took the blame. They both ended up getting grounded from swimming without life jackets. Dani had to get stitches which kept her out of the water until they were removed. But they were sure to do it again as soon as they were out of sight of the adults.

She and her brother had always been close until he got into the drugs. Now, she had no idea where he was or if he was alive. And if he were, would she live to see him again?

Dani dozed once more and dreamed as the child-sized life jacket held her head above water.

She floated along and dreamed she was working after school on the dock to help Uncle Ralph sell what he caught from his fishing boat each day. She did that as a teenager and when she wasn't in school, she helped him on the fishing boat as well. Mom worked in the nursing home in Corpus Christi cleaning bedpans and changing sheets to bring in enough money to keep the family going. Dani's father, Nick, left not long after Cody was born leaving the three of them to fend for themselves.

Dani remembered her mother telling them that she, Nina, and their father, Nick, grew up together. They were inseparable. Even their names went together. And when they graduated high school, they got married. It just seemed like the thing to do. They were a couple before they were old enough to even know what that meant, so they had a backyard wedding on Saturday, and he went to work on Monday. Nina was already pregnant, and Nick went to work on a fishing boat. He had to earn a living now that school was over, and he was a husband.

And the fishing boat was where the trouble started. The fishermen were men, and he was just a boy. They had lived in faraway and exciting places, and Nick had only lived on the gulf coast. He soon realized as he watched Nina's belly swell the second time, he wanted more. He'd heard enough about exotic places in the world that he'd never seen. Never would. And on his next payday, he took a few clothes with him when he left for work and never returned.

Nina's job at the convenience store didn't bring in

much money but she did the best she could until she got on at the nursing home, and then the baby came. Her neighbor babysat for Dani while she worked, and then Cody when he was born, and she went back to work sooner than was recommended. But she had bills to pay.

Uncle Ralph helped out when he could, always saying if he could find Nick, he'd string him up. But he never came back home.

Nina wanted a better life for her children than she could afford, but somehow, that had not happened. They had a happy home life, mostly due to their time spent near the sea with Ralph, but as far as money was concerned, there was little.

Uncle Ralph had been a smoker all his life. He never smoked inside but he always had an ashtray on the deck of the houseboat and probably on his boat when he was out fishing. He knew lung cancer was probably in his future. But he also worked hard in the sun without sunscreen and often with a cigarette hanging out of his mouth as he pulled in the nets. Some form of cancer was inevitable. He was in the best shape of his life, he always said. And he was strong. But not strong enough to ward off cancer. In the end, the treatments took him down and he had to sell his fishing boat to pay the bills. He spent the remaining months of his life on the houseboat

About the time Dani graduated from high school, her uncle took a turn for the worse. He couldn't stay home alone and since the boat and fishing were now a thing of the past, so was Dani's job. She moved in with Uncle Ralph to take care of him and soon found a job on the dock helping the manager collect the rent. She eventually ended up managing the dock when her boss moved on.

Dani and her mom, Nina, took turns taking care of Uncle Ralph. Their run-down apartment only held the two of them. By then Cody was out of the house and running with a rough crowd. He'd quit school and was never home. It drove their mother crazy, but it was how things were.

Dani's mother worked running back and forth from her apartment, to work, to Ralph's, in her broken-down Toyota. Until she hit a guardrail late one night, traveling from work to Ralph's houseboat to relieve Dani. Her death was instantaneous—and seemed to speed up Ralph's.

Just the two of them then, Uncle Ralph asked Dani to write his will on a piece of paper as he dictated it, and he'd sign it.

"Uncle Ralph, it's not fair. What about Cody? He should also own this houseboat," she said quietly.

"No, Cody has to grow up and you deserve this. You've worked for it." He signed with a shaky hand.

It was legal though gut wrenching.

Dani buried both her mother and her uncle within weeks of each other and then cleaned out the apartment with a garage sale since she had no way to make the rent. She took only her clothes and moved into Uncle Ralph's houseboat full time and saw her brother now and then. He hadn't attended either of the funerals. But still Cody was mad about Dani inheriting "his" boat.

A wave hit Dani in the face, and she woke once more, lifting her head. She looked in the direction of shore. The currents were pushing her the right way, which was good, because she couldn't do it herself. Her life jacket was still holding her up. Tonight, she had no desire to see the bottom of the ocean as she once had as a child.

Staring out into the night sky she once more saw the lights and knew they were getting closer. She was headed to the shore if she could stay alive that long. Then something else caught her eye. As the clouds parted in the moonlight, she saw something tall off to the left. A ship? No, it was too small, but there was something sticking out of the water. Her addled brain could not make sense of what she viewed until she heard the bell. It sounded familiar. She'd heard it before. And then it hit her—a buoy that marked the outer edges of the sandbar. It had recently been placed there to get the attention of boaters, and it had a warning bell. The sandbar she had waded recently, and was causing boaters trouble, might just be her savior.

She was near the island!

Holding on to the life jacket she kicked with exhausted legs in the direction of the bell stopping several times along the way. She had to get there. From the buoy she could hang on until someone found her, even if she wasn't found until morning.

A wave washed over her head again causing her to choke but moved her forward. She was determined not to pass out. Her body was used up and her mind was playing tricks on her. Maybe the buoy was an illusion, and she laid her head back down. Suddenly her elbow bumped up against something cold and hard. The buoy. She grabbed it with one shaking hand hanging on to the precious life jacket with the other and wrapped her legs around the rough metal cylinder. It was slimy on the bottom but rough up high above the water line. Her shaky arm reached up toward the top and her fingers found a handhold. Another wave hit her slapping the strap from the life jacket against her face. It startled her but she slowly realized she could use the strap to secure herself to the buoy. Her arms couldn't hold out much longer.

Chapter 33

The hallucinations started with colors. The sea swirled around Cody in colors that weren't on any wheel. And he smiled causing the blisters on his face to crack. The burns were probably benefiting from the salt in the water, but who knew what else was invading his raw skin. Salt wasn't the only thing that lived there. In the water that swirled like an oil slick, he saw the colors slowly become familiar as they created a shape. It was Dani! She was alive and she was there to rescue him. He reached for her and slowly began to sink.

"Dani," he called as she sank back into the water that had become blacker than the night.

At a snail's pace, Cody felt his strength leaving his extremities. From above his body, he watched himself slowly sink as he reached for his sister who was not really there. The massive fin was sliding through his hands, and he was unable to hang on. His head and arms burned as the blisters popped and raw skin was assaulted by salt water. The pain was what kept him awake and even that wasn't working anymore. He knew he was about to pass out and if he did, he'd drown. Maybe he wasn't going to make it after all. How could he let Dani down this way? He had plans for himself—for them. He couldn't just die now with all they'd been through.

That was his last conscious thought as his arm slid down the length of the dolphin and his face sank into the dark water burning his raw skin. His legs followed suit, and his body began its descent.

When the dolphin no longer felt the weight of his passenger, he turned around and immediately dove under the sinking body. He pushed Cody up to the surface and rolled him over, using his nose under the man's shoulder.

Though unconscious, Cody instinctively opened his mouth to breathe the oxygen above the water. He floated in the ocean's salty brine as the waves tossed him about. Scar stayed by his side and gently nudged him forward now and then as he floated along like plankton. Cody had no idea he was being saved as he lay in the dark water and breathed the life-giving oxygen from the night sky. But his savior never left his side as he was gently shoved forward. Scar could use the currents to his advantage and get Cody to safety.

As Cody floated unconscious in the ocean he dreamed of a time when he was a boy, and his sister was tasked with keeping him safe. He felt her jostle him forward now and then to get him back home to Mom and the dinner that awaited them. She had no idea where he had wandered off to, but Dani found him as usual and was bringing him home.

"Cody, Mom's gonna kill me if we don't get home soon. I told you not to wander off. Now we're gonna be late for supper. Why don't you listen and do what you're told now and then?" Dani griped at him but still wrapped her arm around his shoulder lovingly. She'd found him with his foot stuck under the tree root and his shoe untied. He wasn't supposed to be at this vacant lot, which was why he felt the need to be there. He'd seen it when his mom drove past in the car. He'd been told it was dangerous and to stay away. The danger was what made him want to be there. And as soon as he could get away, he found his way back remembering the way his mom had driven when they passed by it. He had promised himself he'd return, and he did.

The lot had a large tree laying mostly on the ground with the roots still attached. A survivor, the tree continued to leaf out on one side and made for a great hiding place. Next to it was the hole where the basement of a house had once been—now, it was just a hole dug in the dirt. Cody wanted to climb down into the hole, but for once he used his head and realized if he got down there, he might not get back up.

Instead, he decided to climb the tree. Being short, Cody had trouble climbing trees, but this one was just at the right height for him. And climb it he did, until he fell and his foot caught in the ragged roots that stuck out of the ground. He wasn't hurt, though he had a scape on his elbow, but that wasn't important. What was important was that it was getting dark, and he was stuck. He'd pulled every direction and was in the process of taking off his tennis shoe when he heard Dani calling him.

"Dani!" he called back. "I'm stuck!"

She rounded the corner and ran to where he waved at her. "Why do you always do what you are told not to do? Mom will be mad, you know," she said as she yanked on his foot then pulled his shoe off. It fell into the bottom of the deep hole, and they watched as it tumbled out of sight. But he was free, even though he had to walk home with only one shoe. What would he tell Mom? She wasn't going to be happy if she had to buy him new shoes. So, he limped home wondering what to tell her with Dani by his side. She always came through for him and he knew she always would.

Cody gasped, realizing he was dreaming and something was shoving on his foot. His shoe was gone—or maybe it had been gone for a while. But the insistent shoving moved up his body and under his arm pushing him forward. The dolphin was still with him. He smiled as he looked into the dark sky and the skin on his face cracked. His face and hands burned, and he looked around. He thought he saw lights in the distance just as a wave washed over him and he choked. The strong rubbery body shoved past him again and he tried to grab its fin, but he couldn't hold on for more than a second. He once more drifted off into unconsciousness.

And dreamed about home.

Life had been tough for them growing up. Mom was always at work and he and his sister stayed with the neighbor when she was gone. He hated the title babysitter. He wasn't a baby. He was the man of the family though Mom and Dani didn't think so. He wore hand-me-downs to school, and he hated that too. The older boys were always making fun of him. What he loved was his time spent at Uncle Ralph's. He was taught to love the ocean, catch fish, and swim off the dock. What Uncle Ralph didn't teach him was how to not be the baby of the family with his mom and sister always telling him what to do. He could decide that for himself.

At home he was the baby, but out on his own, he found he really liked girls. Not his mother and sister, but real girls, the kind you could kiss, and they thought you were cool. Soon, he learned to bat his eyelashes at them and smile just right, and they would do anything he wanted. He had no money so dating wasn't in the cards, but he could normally get them to buy him a taco or something—just for his company. He learned to be charming because he realized it got him places he couldn't go without it.

He had a few jobs, mostly running errands for people. He'd deliver packages for some guys in Corpus Christi and soon it became obvious that he was needed during the week as well as the weekend. School was a bother and going to Uncle Ralph's was in his way, so he quit school and left home long before his sister. She always stayed and helped Mom. Cody had things to do and people who depended upon him. He wasn't a baby anymore.

Most of the time he ignored Dani's calls but when she just kept trying to contact him, he gave in and answered. "Mom's dead," she said sobbing.

Cody was broke as usual so he just didn't bother showing up for his mother's funeral. Dani would expect him to help pay and he didn't want her to know how bad things had gotten for him.

Uncle Ralph couldn't attend their mother's funeral. He seldom got out of bed by then; and then he wrote the hand-written will. Cody didn't attend either funeral.

When she did hear from him, Dani told Cody he could stay with her anytime he wanted. "I'm thinking about buying a tour boat and then you could take my job managing the dock."

Hand-me-downs again. That's when he decided not to go back—unless he was so stoned he couldn't find his way home, wherever that was. Then he and Dani really began to argue.

****

Joey woke in his car to the smell of fishy water and he almost gagged. Corpus smelled fishy sometimes too, but he didn't spend much time this close to the water.

Then he remembered he was at the dock. He looked around and discovered he was finally alone. He could see no one on the dock. That meant he'd run out of time. He had to do the deed whether he wanted to or not.

He stepped out into the night and the breeze cooled his body. His shirt stuck to him, and he smelled like mosquito repellant—or maybe that was his own body odor. It was hard to tell. He'd been cooped up in the car too long. The breeze felt good, and the clouds covered the full moon, most of the time. Complete cloud cover would be nice. They could provide some camouflage in case anyone was up at this hour and hanging out at the dock.

He opened the trunk lid and found the two gasoline cans were still upright. He had wedged them next to the aging spare tire that looked too flat to be useful if he needed it to support the car. At least it accomplished the job of holding the gas cans upright. Lifting the cans from the trunk he closed the lid quietly, still suspicious he wasn't alone. No one came near and he heard no footsteps, so he began his trek to the dock. He carried both gas cans to the middle of the dock and then continued on with just one. He stood trying to decide just how close to get his line of gasoline to the fuel tanks where the tour boats and tourists filled up. He had no idea how far flames could jump, but he wanted to be sure he was nowhere in sight when it happened. As soon as he lit the line of gasoline, he would be history. He'd hide out somewhere on the crappy little strip of sand until the ferry left in the morning since he had no boat to get back to the mainland. But the sooner he got off the island, the better.

He stopped several yards from the little fuel station

and looked once more down the dock at the boats in their slips. "Say goodbye," he said to the boats then pulled the cap from the nozzle of the gas can and tipped it forward. It splashed out onto the toe of his shoe.

"Shit!" he hissed as he shook his toe to get the gasoline off. He hoped it would evaporate before he set the trail on fire. But would it really evaporate, or would it be a source for the flames to take off? He didn't need a hot foot. He could run just fine, thank you.

Tipping the can once more he backed toward the end of the dock. Suddenly his foot was on the edge of the wooden dock. Windmilling his arm to regain his balance, he stepped back in. He didn't want to end up in the water. He turned around and walked toward the end of the dock pouring the liquid out along the way until he reached the other can. He tossed the empty container into the ocean then picked up the full one and began once more creating a stream of liquid that would put an end to the commerce and livelihoods of the residents of Sandhill Island.

Reaching the end of the dock, he tossed the second can into the water and stared at his work. Inside his pocket was the book of matches he brought for tonight. He instinctively stepped his gasoline-soaked foot back before he lit the match. He struck the match and watched it bloom into a flame for just a second before he dropped it onto the line of gasoline.

Then he turned and ran.

****

With a foothold on the lip of the buoy, Dani pushed herself up out of the water holding the life jacket between her and the metal cylinder until she found a tiny shelf she could almost straddle. She wrapped the strap around her waist and the metal cylinder, then snapped it shut. The child-sized life jacket was once more her savior. If she got out of this alive, she would never be without it.

Her arms and legs were scraped from the rough metal and the shelf she sat on gouged her thighs, but she didn't care. She was out of the water and could wait there to be rescued. Surely someone would see her come morning. Her arms no longer had to support her while the little strap held up. She rested her head against the rough metal and looked into the distance then began to shiver. How long until daylight she wondered and struggled to stay awake her eyelids heavy.

When a fireball erupted, lighting up the sky. Was that the dock?

Chapter 34

Skaggs hadn't been in law enforcement for a long time, but he thought it was what he wanted to do with his life. However, he'd like a little more action than he got on Sandhill Island. He'd find a bigger market, but he hated to leave Riggs by himself. Maybe if they had someone else, or if he knew someone who wanted a quieter life or was just getting started. But so far that hadn't happened. He was tired of being number two in the office, but Riggs was good to work with. He might not find that in a bigger city. But right now, he was into detective work. He was going to get to the bottom of what had happened to Dani and Cody. Not having answers made him itch. And he intended to scratch that itch.

Inside the tiny police station, the night constable, Skaggs, called residents of the island to see if anyone had recently seen the Browns. It was late and several times he woke someone, but the island people were happy to help. Sarge snored noisily in the corner oblivious of the action taking place around him as Skaggs brewed coffee. Unlike Sarge, Skaggs thought it was great to be in on the action for once.

Several times Skaggs called Jimmy who ran the fuel pumps at the end of the dock—but the phone continued to ring with no answer. It was unusual that the dock was unmanned but the guy needed a break now and then.

Just as he hung up the phone, the fire alarm blasted.

Skaggs ran from his desk and threw open the door. The island had a tiny volunteer fire department on site and if things got too bad, they called Corpus Christi for reinforcements. That had never happened since Skaggs had worked there. This day was getting more and more exciting. Then he checked himself. He didn't want his neighbors to lose property. But a fire?

The shrill tone of the alarm rang in the constable's office just as it did at the fire department. They had insisted it be installed there too because law enforcement and the fire department worked hand in hand. Sarge lifted his fuzzy head and looked around. A low growl began in the back of the animal's throat.

"It's okay, Sarge. I'll check to see what's going on."

The constable stepped outside to see residents running toward the fire station when his vision was pulled to the bright fireball on the other side of the island. It came from the direction of the dock.

Was their dock on fire?

He ran for the cruiser. Sarge's growl had turned into a howl and just as the constable was about to close the door leaving the animal inside, he thought better of it. What if the fire spread and Sarge needed to escape. He knew of no other reason the dog would leave the security of his home. But just in case, he left the door ajar so Sarge could leave if he needed to. And he raced for the vehicle.

"You'd better stay here, boy," he called back over his shoulder.

He found he wasn't able to park very close with all the other traffic, so he parked and began to run. Weaving through pedestrians who were either there for the show, or had a boat tied up at the pier, the officer ran for the dock. Boat owners were trying in vain to get to their boats and untie them if they weren't already engulfed in flames.

Grabbing his cell phone he called the shrimper, Paul Smith. He had a water cannon on that shrimper, and he knew Paul would help.

The firetruck screamed toward the dock with the volunteers riding on it. The firemen immediately jumped into action as soon as the truck was close enough. Hoses connected, they began to spray the flames. People ran toward the dock on the opposite side and jumped onto boats and in some cases, just cut them lose to float away. They could take their chances out in the water to be rescued later.

The constable knew the safety of the dock was important to the residents of the island. Their businesses and some of their homes were tied to it. They had to save it.

****

Joey almost made it to the end of the dock before his foot slipped and he tumbled down on one knee. He reached for the rope that tied a small boat to the dock and grabbed it just as momentum tossed him forward. The rest was a blur. His hand sported rope burns from grabbing the lifeline as it slipped through his fingers. He hit the dark, fish-smelling water face first and could see nothing. The moon had gone behind a cloud when he surfaced, and he landed between two small boats. He was in the water he hated so much, and he had no idea how to get out.

Kicking to keep his head above water, his foot hit something underwater and he froze. What was in there with him? He'd seen movies where monsters come out of the water, and he didn't plan to die that way. He didn't plan to die at all!

Above him flames swept down the wharf and he began to hear commotion as people ran toward the dock. Should he shout for help, or try to remain hidden?

The dock was built on piers that held it out of the water, and they were slimy from being constantly wet. He reached out a hand and recoiled at the feel of the moss growing on what might be his only savior. Then he stumbled again on something under the water. Flames were getting closer and the two small boats clanged together, catching him in between. He grabbed the edge of one, smashing his fingers and stumbled toward the water's edge scraping his ankle on whatever was under the water. He was near the bank but had no idea what kind of junk was on the bottom. He could climb over it using the boat to hang on to or try to shimmy up the slimy pier. He doubted he could shimmy. But feeling the heat of the fire on his face, he needed to get out of there! Holding on to the boat, he attempted to climb up the bank when suddenly a hand was in his face.

"Grab hold!" a man in a police uniform called.

Joey stopped. Water dripped from his brow and he thought he was about to get arrested, then imagining the alternatives in the water—he reached out.

The officer yanked him out onto the bank and then ran toward the fire. Joey was left to thank his lucky stars he was alive and not in jail. He was soaked in smelly fish water. At least the gasoline was rinsed off his shoe and he hadn't been arrested.

He tried to remain unnoticed but walked quickly for his car that sat in the parking lot. Reaching in his pocket for the key fob—he came up empty. He felt both pockets and even in the back. He never put his car keys in his back pocket, but it was worth a try. He stopped in the middle of the road and felt all his pockets once more. He turned and looked at the water and realized he couldn't dive in to find the fob. First, he hated the water, and second, he couldn't swim. Besides, how would he see if he did go looking for it? The key to this car was in the water somewhere. How could this night get any worse?

Maybe he left it unlocked and he could hotwire it. Hotwire his own car. That was funny—and it wasn't. He walked toward the car that sat at the dark end of the parking lot and tried the door. It would not budge. People ran all around him. He had nothing to break into the piece of junk that he was longing to trade in soon. The windows were now up, and the doors were locked. He was locked out of his own car. His only way home.

He had planned to be parked for the first ferry of the morning and now he had no transportation. He could walk to the ferry and then take the bus when he reached the mainland, but that wasn't an option he liked. He could have the car towed and rekeyed, but that would call a lot of attention. Someone would have to come from Corpus to do that. He'd been wanting a new car anyway. Glancing behind him, he crept off into the night as most of the town ran toward the fire and their boats. He'd find a place to hide until daylight and then he'd get off this tiny island and never have to worry about it again.

Chapter 35

Paul Smith was a longtime resident of Sandhill Island. He owned a shrimp boat, and he provided fresh shrimp to the residents and sometimes places along the gulf coast. He was a big provider for the restaurant, Le Chez. His shrimp and fish combined with Meg's produce made it the premier restaurant anywhere around. He and his wife had lived on the island all their lives. He had a sister, Martha, on the island as well and a niece, Sandy, in Biloxi, Mississippi, who often visited with her kids. He was a staple on Sandhill Island and was always ready and willing to help his neighbors.

Paul stood looking into the night sky from his shrimper. He hated to make his crew work nights, but shrimp had been in short supply lately and he needed a new place to fish. That was when the call came in from the constable on the island. It was garbled, but he thought the man said the dock was on fire. He tried to call back, but they were too far out for good reception.

"Okay, pull 'em in!" he shouted at the crew. "We're headed home. And get something to eat when you're finished. This might still be a long night."

There were groans from the crew. They had worked hard and had little to show for it so far. But he'd make it up to them. If their hometown was in peril, they needed to help. He turned the boat toward shore and began to travel back home as the men pulled in the nearly empty nets. There wouldn't be a lot of shrimp to sell when they got home.

Night runs were rare, and they hadn't been out that long but the distance to the island was still substantial. He had plenty of fuel, planning to be out a while, and he had plenty of food to feed his crew, but he hadn't planned on this turnaround.

"Jake, I got a call from the constable on the island, and I think he said the dock was on fire. I'm trying to call him back. But in the meantime, get the water cannon ready to go. We're headed home."

Jake, the oceanographer who worked for Paul when he wasn't out mapping the ocean floor, nodded and headed to the pump. Paul knew he could count on Jake for anything that needed to be done. He'd been a good hand and had once risked his life delivering strawberries for his girlfriend. A water cannon was small potatoes to Jake. It essentially pulled water from the ocean and sprayed it wherever it was needed. It could be used to put out fires onboard other vessels or on the shore. If Paul heard the phone call right and they were needed at home, they would get there as soon as possible. He continued to call the constable's office as they traveled.

The closer they got to the island the more obvious it was that the light around the dock was much brighter than normal. Paul was afraid he had heard the phone call right. The dock was on fire.

"Get that cannon ready to go!" Paul shouted.

The big shrimper made good time coming into shore, and between the lights on the dock and the fire, Paul was able to see the comings and goings of the people trying to get their boats to safety. This was their livelihood, and for some of them, the boats were their home.

The wind suddenly changed directions and increased. If this kept up, the dock wouldn't be the only thing that caught fire.

****

Billie Stone woke to the sound of sirens, something unusual on Sandhill Island. But with her windows open and the sea breeze flowing through it was hard not to hear it. A fire on a little island like her hometown was something to be concerned about. She ran to the front porch and saw that the fire was coming from the direction of the dock. Neil's boat was tied up there!

She couldn't believe he slept through the noise. He still lay snoring on his side of her bed.

"Neil!" She jerked back the covers. "The dock is on fire! Your boat is in danger."

He seemed confused at first as she dressed and shouted instructions to the man from up north who didn't realize the danger of fire on a small island. Suddenly it hit home with him. Throwing on shorts and tennis shoes, they ran the half mile toward the dock where people were gathering. The volunteer fire department was there hosing down the dock closest to the shore, but parts were unreachable with their hoses. Neil's boat was tied up on the other side of the pier.

The scene was mad chaos as people tried to get to their boats. The ones on fire with no one around were simply cut loose and shoved out into the water with the hopes that they would not float back in and set something else on fire.

String grabbed Billie's arm as he ran past toward where Dani normally moored her boat. "Have you seen Dani?" he called as Neil and Billie ran past. "I can't reach her, and I don't see her boat anywhere!"

"No, we just got here. But I'll tell her to call you if I find her."

Billie and Neil continued down the soggy dock dodging firemen and residents. She could still see his boat tied up. Billie caught an elbow in the ribs from her neighbor and was nearly knocked off the dock as she ran. She quickly grabbed a rope attached to a vessel to regain her balance and then continued to run.

Neil jumped in and started the engine of his vessel. She grabbed the lines on one side and cast them off before running to the other side. "Let's go!" She jumped onto the boat as she untied the last line and gestured that he should back up and leave the slip.

They pulled out into the dark ocean with the moonlight above and fire behind. Neil turned on his running lights as he pulled away. They didn't need to hit another boat and have an accident at a time like this.

That was when they saw the huge shrimper headed their way.

Chapter 36

Dani had given up swatting mosquitoes and gnats that dive-bombed her eyes. She was exhausted and if they found her sucked dry and tied to a buoy in the morning, so be it. Her thighs were raw from hanging on to the buoy and the saltwater stung them. Blood ran down her legs. The waves jostled her, and her eyes were swollen to a point of barely seeing. Her arms still ached, but she continued to remind herself she was alive. She didn't know about Cody.

She sloshed in and out of the water as the buoy tilted back and forth. She could see the bright light near the dock become brighter and then she thought she saw the shrimper with its nets hung on each side in the distance. It was coming home. Maybe they would see her.

She smelled smoke and was certain it was coming from the direction of the dock. She was afraid the unimaginable was happening. Was her dock on fire? Where was *Wanderlust?* And where was Cody?

She knew she was near the sandbar because the buoy she was attached to was placed there to warn boaters to stay away for fear of being beached. Maybe she could untie herself and swim through the shallow water. She had rested some and she had her life jacket to assist her. The thought wandered through her mind as she came and went out of consciousness.

Then she saw the fin in the dark water coming her

way. She'd waded in this water before and encountered a shark. Could it be happening again?

****

"Be careful of the sandbar. It begins on the other side of that buoy," Billie said and pointed to the strange looking obstacle poking out of the water. What was wrong with it? It looked too fat to be a buoy and why was it leaning that way. Something seemed to be hanging onto it.

Neil nodded and pulled out into deeper water.

"Neil, what is that on the buoy? Is that a person?" Billie pointed as she asked her question.

"I don't know, but let's go see." He turned the boat in the direction of the buoy. He couldn't get too close and end up in shallow water. He slowed his engine and coasted closer to the buoy.

Someone was hanging onto the buoy and making it lean in and out of the water.

"Ahoy!" Billie shouted. "Hello?"

She saw movement on the buoy. Was that an arm waving at them?

****

Dani kicked out at the shark as it brushed by her on the buoy. It was checking out the food supply. It was small, but it could still do damage, especially if she were strapped to a buoy and unable to move. Her thumbs were numb as she tried to loosen the strap that had saved her life many times that day. The plastic thumb latch hung tight as she tried to release it. Barely able to see, she thought the fin had turned and was coming back.

Then she saw the boat. Someone was shouting and it was headed her way.

The rough hide of the shark scraped her calf peeling

away skin and someone began to scream. Maybe it was her. The strap around her held tight and she twisted and shrieked trying to get loose. It was almost daylight. Had she survived this long to only run into a shark this close to home? This time the shark attacked head on—mouth open.

"No, you don't!" she yelled. She had not come this far to be eaten by a shark on her own beach. She kicked out again and grazed a tooth with a bare ankle. Then something blunt hit her leg. It was an oar. She struggled pulling and punching the thumb latch on the life jacket but to no avail—when the boat pulled up alongside her. Large hands reached down, and a knife cut the strap. Instinctively she latched onto the life jacket as she was hoisted onboard the boat. She heard someone shouting and slapping the shark in the water with an oar. She was pulled into the boat and thankfully placed on a bench. The life jacket was still clutched to her chest. It was the last thing she remembered until she was awakened and offered water.

"That little shark was determined," the woman's voice said as she laid the oar down on the bottom of the boat. The man again offered her water and suggested she drink as the woman held her head up. Then she heard the woman call and say they found her. And Dani was fairly certain that she was her. Someone had been looking for her!

Dani was almost dozing when she was once more awakened by the stinging on her leg as bandages were wrapped around the gash. She drank once more then passed out peacefully as she was covered by the warmth of a beach towel.

Chapter 37

Paul stood at the front of his boat ready to give the order. His island was burning. "Jake, fire up that water cannon. And keep those tanks wet. We don't want that fuel going up. The fire department can handle the rest of the dock. I'll steady the shrimper." He stood at the helm and tried to keep the front of the boat pointed toward the island while the waves worked against him.

Jake aimed the nozzle of the water cannon at the dock, determined not to let the fire get to the fuel pumps. "Grab hold of the hose, boys. This is gonna get dicey." Several of the fisherman grabbed the back end of the hose to keep Jake on his feet when he let the water pressure go. He opened the nozzle and aimed at the pier soaking the fuel tanks first and then keeping the fire at bay. The tanks were waterproof in a storm, so they should be okay with a little water spraying from a nozzle. And there was no danger of running out of water since the shrimper was sucking saltwater in from the ocean and spraying it out onto the dock.

The volunteer fire department pulled up at the other end of the dock. The one truck that the island owned attached their hose to the hydrant. The city's water hydrant was fed by lines from fresh, potable water. It came from an aquifer under the island, and sometimes it wasn't enough. Citizens were often told to boil their drinking water and many bought bottled water to be sure they had enough. And now they needed everything they had to put out a fire.

Corpus Christi Fire Department had been called, and the ferry was ready to transport their fire trucks which contained onboard water tanks to help. They were on the way, but time was of the essence.

Just when it was not needed, the wind kicked up waves that sloshed onto the shore and the dock. The waves did little to put out the gasoline-driven fire on the wooden dock. Instead, it blew burning embers toward the mainland, across the island, and headed to the downtown and residential areas. Residents were using garden hoses to fight the fires, draining the city's water and emptying what was stored in the fire truck. The little island only had so much fresh water available. The Coast Guard couldn't get there fast enough. They too had sea water cannons like Paul's shrimper and would not run out of water.

Boats free floated in the port of the marina, some on fire. Several had been shoved into the shallow water by waves that beached them as they blew sideways and stuck them on the newly formed sandbar. Where was the Coast Guard?

Sam dug a well years ago when city water wasn't as available as now. He and Meg both needed wells for their gardens, and when she had one drilled, he decided to do the same. Sam had a small herb garden, but he also wanted to be sure he had enough water for the restaurant. He attached his well to a purifier to use for cooking. And it was about to come in handy as long as the aquifer underneath the island didn't run dry.

He had helped untie the boats to get them free from the dock until it became obvious he was in the way. Then he stood on the deck of his restaurant, where the piano sat on nights they had live music, and watched the embers float through the sky—blowing toward town.

Many of his neighbors with larger boats had moved them to his small dock. Some just sat on their boats out in the harbor staying away from the fire. The smaller boats were just beached on the sand for later retrieval.

****

Sam watched his neighbors wondering where he was needed most. Boats floated unmanned out in the harbor, but out of danger of the flames. Unless the wind shifted. The air was acrid with smoke, burning his eyes and nose. Even from a distance his bare arms felt the heat coming off the dock. Embers floated in the air, and he pulled a bandana from his pocket and covered his nose and mouth. He kept them in his pocket for when he cooked and had wiped the sweat from his brow earlier. Even though he was used to the heat in a kitchen, he still didn't want to drip perspiration into the food while he cooked, so he always kept one with him. Now it was going to come in handy once more.

His eyes blurred with tears, and he tried not to cough. He walked toward the water untying the bandana as he went. He leaned over and dipped it in the water, then wiped his face and neck. Once more rinsing it, he wrung it out and again tied it around his face to filter out the smoke. He couldn't cover his eyes, but he would, if he could have. Then he saw the spark blossom and land at the end of the deck. It settled on the linen curtains used to shade the outdoor dining from the daily sun. Flames blew up immediately multiplying into an inferno.

His own deck was on fire!

He grabbed the water hose and turned it on to drown

the flames, just in time to see a spark take another corner. The curtains they had put up for shade and to make the deck homey quickly caught the ones hanging next to them. At this rate, his restaurant was going to be destroyed. He hosed down the curtains in front of him and then began to spray the next. They were linen and helped hide the sun when it was warm, but now they only helped feed the flames.

When it became clear that he wouldn't be able to save the curtains, he concentrated on spraying the door to the restaurant itself. He couldn't lose it. It was all he had in the world, and he had employees who depended upon it for a livelihood as much as he did.

Once the entrance to the restaurant was extinguished, he turned when he heard the whoosh behind him. The last set of curtains caught fire just as the water pressure began to drop. He was out of water. With all the residents soaking their own homes and the hydrant attached to the fire truck, they had overstressed the small water system on the island. He ran to the curtains and ripped them from the rods, throwing them out into the sand. Then he danced a jig on the flames to put the rest of them out. After he could see no spark, he scooped sand on top to smother any flames left.

As the last of the sand was scooped, String ran up breathless. "Have you seen Dani? Her boat is gone, and I can't reach her."

Sam looked up at the tall man, then stood and brushed the sand from his hands. "No, but the police are looking for her. She didn't work for me tonight. She said she had a tour. They went out looking for her boat."

"Let me know if you see her," he called and then ran off down the beach.

Later, Sam would discover the blisters on his hands and that the fire had melted his tennis shoes. They were a small price to pay for saving Le Chez.

But where was Dani?

Suddenly the most beautiful sound in the world hit Sam's ears.

Sirens coming from the other side of the island screamed that the Corpus Christi Fire Department had arrived. The ferry had made good time, even against the winds, bringing the fire trucks from the mainland to help. These trucks were tankers with their own water supply, up to 2600 gallons each. And they were going to be needed.

The commander jumped from the front truck as they pulled up at the dock. One group immediately pointed their nozzles at the dock that still flamed. He turned to the second group and said, "Take those trucks to the residential area and see what needs to be doused."

They raced away to the other side of the island to see what needed to be done. In no time the dock was drenched and the last of the flames were extinguished. The smell of smoke still hung in the air, but the dock was only partially gone. Most importantly, the fuel tanks were intact.

Just as the flames were subsiding, Riggs and Agent Murphy arrived with *Wanderlust* in tow tying up in front of Le Chez. The main dock would not be used for a long time—if ever. They tied up the patrol boat and then untied *Wanderlust* and tethered it to a slot of its own. It was still in good condition, just out of fuel, and they knew Dani would be happy to see it—wherever she was.

"Wow, it looks like a war zone here," Riggs said as he surveyed the damage. Pieces of wood floated by as the sky started to drizzle. The winds had blown in precipitation that helped to put out any fires that were still burning.

Agent Murphy nodded. "It actually looks better up close. I was afraid from what we saw out on the water, the whole island was on fire. What would the residents do if they didn't have a way to get off the island?"

A siren of a different kind wailed out on the water and all heads turned. The Coast Guard had finally arrived. They had traveled a longer distance from Corpus Christi since their boats were required to round the end of the island and not come across the strip of water on the ferry like the fire department. It had taken longer, but they had arrived. And they could still be of use.

Riggs turned to the Coast Guard captain and pointed at Carlos. "I need this prisoner transported to Corpus Christi. He stole a boat, and we still have not found the owner. We don't have a name or any identification yet. Agent Murphy, DEA, will tell you everything you need to know about the prisoner." He gestured to Murphy who nodded and walked off with Carlos in handcuffs toward the Coast Guard vessel.

Neil ran his boat up on the sand since the rest of the dock was full. He might need to be pulled back out when things settled down. Seeing the patrol boat, he waved at Riggs and Agent Murphy. They ran to where he had beached the boat to help with whatever needed to be done.

"I have someone who needs medical attention. Dani Brown was found hanging on to a buoy that guards the sandbar. She's in pretty rough shape. A young shark was attacking her when we found her, and she has some abrasions. Mostly, she's exhausted and probably dehydrated. She keeps talking about her brother Cody. But we haven't seen him."

"Dani!" String shouted as he parted the people standing in front of the boat. He pushed his way through and rushed to her side. "Is she going to be okay?" he asked as he brushed her hair from her eyes and then grabbed her hand hanging on tight.

"I think so," said Neil. "The Coast Guard will transport her to the hospital for treatment."

"Thank you both for taking care of her. We've been looking for her," Officer Riggs said. He walked to the bench where Dani lay covered with a beach towel. He leaned over and touched her face. "Good to see you. You're going to be okay, thanks to Neil and Billie. We're going to send you to Corpus to be examined. The Coast Guard will transport you."

Dani shivered and opened her eyes. "Cody," was all she said before passing out again and the Coast Guard medics placed her on a stretcher and took her onboard their boat. She was limp as a rag except for the cast iron grip she had on the life jacket that had saved her life.

String continued to hang on to her limp hand until he was asked to let go by a medic. "We'll take good care of her, sir," the medic said as they took her stretcher away.

"Officer Riggs!" Poppy called as he ran down the small dock that had become the only one in use. Blackie the dog followed close at his heels. "Officer Riggs! Come quick! I think I found Cody!"

Riggs and Murphy followed Poppy as the Coast Guard took possession of their prisoner. For a little guy, Poppy was fast. So many residents of the island had gathered at the dock, it was hard to push their way though. They followed Poppy down the beach to where Dani had waded the day she ran into a shark. String followed the officers.

Poppy instantly ran into the water without stopping and grabbed at something floating there. It looked like a man. He was face up and floating in knee-deep water. His face was blistered and what hair he had floated around him like an oddly styled wig. Most importantly he was breathing. It was hard to tell how old he was, but the little bit of brown hair left on his head said he was young. The dark sky was beginning to pink and the man opened one blue eye. He looked like Cody Brown.

"Cody, is that you?" Riggs asked as the man tried to rouse. A splash out in the water drew Riggs' attention and he saw the fin. Then the dolphin raised its head, smiled, and squeaked then splashed back down. Scar slid under the water and went back to wherever Scar went when he was not near Sandhill Island.

Officer Riggs called for another stretcher.

"Cody," String said, "Dani is going to be so happy to see you."

The dock was salvaged—at least part of it. Dani and Cody were found, and people were milling around checking their boats for damage. They had saved their island. If they hadn't, they'd all be out on their boats or just in the water watching everything burn. They knew they were lucky. It could have been much worse.

Riggs surveyed the damage of his hometown and knew they were safe. He had done all that could be done. "Agent Murphy, I could use a cup of coffee. We have a pot back at the station. Care to join me? I think there is a dog there who might need out or want his breakfast. It was a long night. String, you want some coffee?"

"Thanks, Riggs, another time." String walked away and Riggs knew he would find a way to get to Dani. He knew enough people on the island who could get him to Corpus or he could find his own way.

"I could use a cup of coffee," Murphy said as he stretched and rubbed his back.

The patrol car was gone, so Riggs knew Skaggs had taken it back to the station probably to keep it safe. They could walk. Nothing was too far away on Sandhill Island.

"Looks like we're walking," he said to the DEA agent, and they headed to the station and a much-needed cup of coffee.

When they got there, the cruiser was parked beside the building and the door to the building stood open. They stepped inside and smelled coffee already brewing. It was just the thing after a long night. Sarge lifted his massive head and huffed a greeting, then lay back down.

"Hey, big guy. It was an exciting night. Did you sleep through it? How about a walk?" He'd take Sarge out for a walk and take his coffee to go. With the way most days went, they kept commuter cups ready and available.

"I'll be back. Sarge and I are going for a walk and to survey the damage," he called over his shoulder as he and the big dog walked out the door.

Murphy took his coffee to the chair and made himself at home with his feet on the desk while he sipped. Skaggs, normally the night constable, was already dozing at his station.

Chapter 38

Riggs and Sarge walked across the island looking for damage in the early morning sun. Riggs sipped his coffee while Sarge watered a few plants along the way. Without thinking, Riggs walked toward the place where the ferry docked and loaded four times a day with passengers. Sarge ambled to his favorite place where he often did his serious business near the dumpsters beside the docking area.

Suddenly the big dog began to bark loudly enough to scare most suspects into submission if they had no idea how docile he really was.

"What's wrong, Sarge?" Riggs leaned around the dumpster and saw a man hiding. He wore all black, with dirty black hair that hung in his frightened eyes as he stared at the dog. The man had some holes in his shirt that looked burned.

"Get that thing away from me! I didn't do nothing!" The man attempted to back up, but he was already up against the dumpster.

"What are you doing back here?" Riggs asked.

"Just waiting on the ferry," the man replied still attempting to back away from the dog.

"Well, it's probably not on schedule. Are you burned? Do you need medical attention?"

"No, I'm fine. Like I said, just waiting on the ferry."

"Get back, Sarge," Riggs said and set his coffee cup

down, reached for the man's hand, and pulled him up. When he stepped from behind the dumpster into the light Riggs realized he reeked of gasoline. "Sir, have you been into gasoline? We had a big fire here on the island that started with gasoline. We found the cans in the water next to the dock." He narrowed his eyes at the man and looked him up and down.

The man dressed in black started to run.

Sarge was right behind him. The massive dog took one leap and landed on the man's back, knocking him to the ground. All it took was for the dog to sit on him. The suspect was going nowhere. Riggs caught up with them quickly.

Riggs looked down at the man's face as he screamed for the dog to get off. Sarge just sat. "What's your name?" he asked.

"Get this big oaf off of me!"

"What's your name?"

"Joey."

"Well, Joey, you are under arrest on suspicion of arson." Riggs pulled his handcuffs from his belt and snapped one on Joey's wrist. "Off, Sarge," he said, and the big dog slowly stepped off the suspect who immediately breathed easier. "Come with me to the station," he said snapping the other handcuff on the suspect's wrist as he lay on the ground and pulled him up. Riggs retrieved his coffee, then took his prisoner to the station house with Sarge leading the way.

"Have a seat," Riggs said as he shoved Joey into a chair next to his desk. "Gentlemen, meet Joey. He smells like gasoline, and I found him hiding behind some dumpsters. He says he knows nothing about the fire."

"Hey, I know you," Skaggs said as he took his feet

off the desk. "In fact, I think I pulled you out of the water next to a couple of floating gasoline cans."

Agent Murphy looked him up and down. "And you were there the night Dani Brown's houseboat mysteriously sank."

Riggs' eyes narrowed. "Joey, you're in a heap of trouble."

****

Jimmy had taken the last ferry of the night and found out where the bus service was located. He'd find his way to Joey's and if the man weren't home, he'd wait. It turned out the trip was not far by bus, but no one answered the door of the apartment. Joey didn't know he was coming and must have had other plans.

He waited on the steps of Joey's apartment all night, dozing in the night only awakened by annoying mosquitoes and the occasional car. He was sure Joey would arrive in the morning. When the sun began to rise Jimmy looked across the parking lot and saw men walking his way. They looked homeless or stoned. He didn't like the look of them. They looked desperate and desperate men did desperate things. He stared at them from the grimy steps where he had slept last night, and one finally walked his way.

"Hey, who are you? Have you seen Joey?" the grimmest one of the bunch asked as he approached.

"No, I was waiting on him. He gave me his address. Does he normally stay out all night?" That was a personal question, Jimmy knew, but maybe the man had some information.

The man shrugged. "I don't know, but he's normally here in the morning with the stuff. Can you get it? I have the cash."

That was when Jimmy realized this was how it went. The junkies showed up and Joey sold to them. He'd do it himself if he knew where the stuff was stored. That would show initiative, wouldn't it? But he didn't know where Jimmy kept it. He'd just have to wait.

"I wish I could, man. I was just supposed to meet Joey here. Sorry." He really was sorry. He could help his new boss out if he knew where the product was stored. "I guess he'll show up eventually."

The man went back and sat on the curb with the others and Jimmy stared off into the morning sun as his stomach grumbled. He didn't know when Joey would be coming.

****

Paul's shrimper had to stay out in deeper water; the small docks left unharmed would not hold his deep boat. So, they used the lifeboats to come up on shore leaving the shrimper anchored. The men were tired and ready to go home and since the fire was out, there was no reason for them to stay on the shrimper. Paul cleaned out the galley and brought the food he had planned to feed the crew. He sent ice chests to shore with the men in the boats that came out to meet him. In the last boat, Paul brought what little catch they had before they returned home to help with the fire. It was mostly shrimp since they sorted and threw back fish that were caught in their drag nets. As he pulled his boat up on shore, he looked at Le Chez. The curtains on the deck of the restaurant were charred, but the restaurant itself appeared to be okay. He waved at Sam who was pulling down burned curtains and shoving them in a trash can.

Sam walked his way, brushing soot from his body, and then reached out to shake Paul's hand. "Thank you and your crew for keeping those fuel tanks from exploding. This island might not have survived if that had happened."

"We were glad to help. I just wish we could have gotten here sooner. We were out at sea when the call came in. We came as soon as we could. I have a little shrimp, not much. Do you want it?" Paul gestured toward the boat he had just pulled up on shore. "And I have a bunch of food for the crew that didn't get eaten."

"I doubt anyone will feel much like dining tonight. But what if we combine resources and offer a picnic to the residents who helped out here. We could feed the Coast Guard too, at least the ones still here. And of course the Corpus Fire Department if they'll stay."

It didn't take long for the rumor to spread that Paul and Sam were cooking on the shore. Residents of the island brought side dishes and whatever they had from home. An impromptu meal fit for a king began to be assembled. Tables were dragged out from the restaurant, but many people spread picnic blankets on the sand. Meg and Alex showed up with a blackberry cobbler and enough sliced tomatoes to feed the entire island. Her garden was in its glory, and she was happy it didn't burn. They all thanked the fire department, Coast Guard, and Paul, for saving their homes. They ate a beautiful breakfast picnic on the beach they loved so well as people told stories of the night before.

Chapter 39

Dani remembered little of the trip to the hospital. She was in and out of consciousness but held tightly to the child-sized life jacket that had been her savior. A kindly nurse finally convinced Dani to let her hold it long enough for the doctor to assess her injuries. She promised to return it as soon as he was finished.

The doctor walked back in with her chart to find her hugging the still wet PFD. "I think you are going to be fine, Ms. Brown." He was the doctor lucky enough to be on call in the Corpus Christi emergency room early that morning. "You have some abrasions and dehydration but with what you've been through, you're lucky to be alive. Most people would not have survived that ordeal. We're going to keep you overnight and let you get some rest. You should be out of here tomorrow."

"Cody," she croaked, her mouth still dry no matter how much she drank.

"Your brother has suffered some burns. He is being treated, and from what I hear he will be fine also. He was on a different boat than you, right?"

Dani cleared her throat as much as she could. "Yes, we were on different boats. Doctor, Cody is an addict. I wanted to be sure you knew that. And after he is released, I want to get him into a rehabilitation facility. Can you help me with that?"

"I'll talk to the doctor treating him and we'll see

about making some arrangements." Dani dozed off again and soon was roused and told she was being transported to a regular room. She wanted to go home. But as long as she was here, she was close to Cody.

Her hospital room was cozy with lavender wallpaper and a bed that was more comfortable than what she'd had on her houseboat—the one that sank. She hardly remembered the one in her apartment since she only spent a few nights there. When she got back there, she would see to it that the door to the apartment locked as it should.

The nurse checked on her, refilling her water jug, and then left. It didn't take long for Dani to doze off again, probably due to the drugs in the IV that stuck out of her arm. When they first wheeled her in, her arms still ached from hanging on to *Wanderlust* and the life jacket. Her legs cramped in ways she had never felt—until the muscle relaxers they gave her kicked in. And when they did, it was the last thing she remembered—and she slept through the night.

"Good morning!" the perky nurse said as she checked Dani's vital signs.

Dani woke up groggy with bright sunshine in her eyes and tried to sit. The fluorescent lights and constant noise were a dead giveaway that she was still in the hospital. She wanted coffee, and quiet. She might get the latter if she were lucky—probably not the former.

"How are we feeling this morning?" the nurse continued.

Dani realized she wasn't in pain and that was a good thing. "Well, I don't know how you're feeling but I'm feeling like I would love some coffee. And do you know when I'll be able to get out of here?" Maybe she was being rude, but she just wanted to go home.

The woman continued to smile. This was not her first grumpy patient. "Well, the breakfast cart is right outside in the hall, and I'll check on that coffee. When you get to go home, however, is up to the doctor."

"Well, when do you think he'll be in?" she asked.

"I don't know. You're not his only patient but I'm sure he'll be in soon." She rolled in the breakfast tray and then left.

First thing in the morning, Dani needed a bathroom, and this morning was no different except that she had to take the IV pole with her and try to keep her hospital gown closed. Where were her clothes, anyway? It was a slow process, but she found she moved slowly this morning anyway, with or without the IV. Her muscles still ached and might for a while. At least she moved.

She was starving. She hadn't eaten breakfast yesterday (was that only yesterday?). In fact, had she eaten all day? Maybe she was given something in the ER, but she couldn't remember. However, she knew she wanted to eat. Breakfast was the standard scrambled eggs and toast, but the coffee was wonderful. She had no idea how much she wanted coffee until she lifted the cover and smelled it. It was the nectar of the gods. She'd need a second cup but instead she drank the ice water in the thermos container that sat on her tray. It was a miracle it was still cold.

She hadn't spent much time in a hospital, but she remembered there were drawers and closets that might hold her clothes. She began to search. A small free-standing closet was in the corner. Maybe her clothes were in there. She walked to the closet with her new best friend, the IV pole, by her side and opened the door. A fishy odor hit her in the face. There were no clothes—but the life jacket that was her constant companion at sea was hanging there. In the bottom of the closet was a pile of sand that might have fallen off the floatation device but where were her clothes? Maybe they threw them away since they were soaked with salt water. But they weren't in her closet.

"You're up, I see," said a voice at the door.

She had company.

"String, Constable Riggs! It's good to see you both. Yes, I'm fine and ready to go home. Where do you think they put my clothes?" She pulled at the cloth in the back of her gown hoping it was closed. Just in case, she kept the front side of her body toward her visitors.

String smiled. "I don't know. Have you seen the doctor? I don't think you can go home until you're released."

Almost on cue nurse sunshine reappeared. "I have come to take your IV out. You don't need it anymore and that should make you more comfortable." She laid folded clothes on the bed.

Dani walked to the bed and there on the sheets were her shorts, tee shirt, and underwear she'd worn in the ocean for all those hours. "Are those my clothes that I came in wearing?"

"We washed them for you. Now if you will sit on the bed, I'll get that IV out. Then you'll just have to wait on the doctor."

"Thank you so much. Whatever is in that IV, I need to drink it on a daily basis. I don't know when I've felt this rested and lucky."

"Sounds to me like you are lucky to be alive," she said as she slid the needle out of Dani's arm and covered it with a sterile bandage and colorful adhesive wrap. "Your brother is here, too, and you could go see him if you like. You still have time before the doctor sees you. He might not be in until after lunch."

Dani's face fell at the thought of not being released for a while.

String cleared his throat and nodded toward the bathroom. "Go change and we'll find Cody."

Dani padded down the hall in the non-skid socks the hospital had provided, and her scratchy shorts and tee shirt that smelled like industrial soap. She had no idea where her shoes were—probably the bottom of the ocean somewhere. But thanks to Meg and Shayla there were more in her apartment. String held her arm as she talked to Riggs, and they walked down the hall. She felt more like herself than she had in some time. She found herself smiling and enjoying the men's company.

"Here we are, Room 412," Riggs said.

And her smile faltered. Was that her brother lying in the bed with bandages on his face and arms?

"Cody!" She ran to his bedside and stared down at him. His face was red and bandaged in places. His beautiful brown shaggy hair had been cut and possibly burned off. He had blisters around his mouth and both arms were wrapped in gauze.

A tear trickled down her cheek as she gazed down at the little brother she used to play in the sand with. Mom said she had to look after him, and now look at him. She had tried so hard to help him, but she had failed.

She leaned her head carefully on his chest and could hear his heart beating and she tried not to cry—but that was impossible. Then she realized he moved and wrapped an arm around her and then a second one.

"Dani," he said in a scratchy voice. "You're alive. I knew if anyone could have survived out there it was you."

She looked up and could see his blue eyes staring back at her and suddenly she sobbed uncontrollably.

"Well, I had help," she said wiping her eyes with the palms of her hands. "There was a life jacket that kept me afloat. The last time I saw you, the cigar boat was speeding away. I thought I'd never see you again."

"I had help, too. Scar. I think he kept me afloat and nudged me toward shore. I'd be dead without him. I really don't remember much except that nose pushing me forward. I owe him more than one bucket of fish."

"It still amazes me that we weren't that far from each other while we were floating at sea. We both ended up on the same sandbar. If I'd known where you were, I could have helped. There were two life jackets, but I could only get one. And the police found *Wanderlust*. She was okay, just out of fuel."

Cody squeezed her hand.

Riggs cleared his throat. "I'd like to hear both of your stories when you are up to it. The island has had a couple of eventful days, and I think you two can fill in a lot of blanks for us. And we are all happy to know you are both alive. The man who stole *Wanderlust* is in custody. So is Joseph Rossi, for arson, attempted murder, drug dealing, and probably a lot of other things. I still don't know how the two are connected."

Dani looked up unwilling to let go of her brother just yet. "We can probably tell you about that."

"Well, that will have to wait," said the nurse who walked in. "I need to change some bandages and try to get this guy to eat something. He just kept asking for his

215

sister. Maybe he'll cooperate a little more now that he has seen her."

Dani stood and grabbed a tissue from Cody's bedside table. "I'll be back later. They're letting me go after lunch, I think. But I'll be back. You eat something and let this woman work her magic, little brother," she said as she backed away not wanting to let go of him.

Cody nodded and a single tear rolled down his face into the bandages.

String pulled Dani away and they walked back down the hall. "I thought we'd completely lost you," he said pulling her close as they walked down the hall. She leaned her head on his arm as they walked. She wanted to be able to stay that way forever.

Riggs stuck around to see what the doctor said and then took Dani and String home to Sandhill Island. She hadn't even thought about how she would get home, but she rode in the cruiser parked on the ferry across the strand of water that separated her home from the mainland. Her arms were wrapped around the life jacket that had saved her. Riggs then drove her to her apartment. She could have walked from the ferry, but she was grateful.

Once home, she stepped into her new apartment and looked around. String was still by her side.

"I can't believe you came to see me in the hospital."

"Like I said, I was worried, but Riggs offered to bring me." He tried to hide a yawn.

"You should go home and get some rest. Maybe we could meet back later?"

He seemed reluctant but yawned once again. "Yeah, you're right. I'll go and you can get some rest too." He squeezed her hand and then walked out the door and toward his end of the island.

She changed into some clothes that smelled more like her than disinfectant, and found some shoes, grabbed a drink from the fridge, then walked down to the dock carrying the life jacket. She was unsure what she planned to do with it, but for now, she was like a two-year-old with a teddy bear and unable to put it down.

She found *Wanderlust* tied up next to the police boat on the dock that belonged to Le Chez. The commercial dock where all the other boats had once been moored was in shambles. She wandered down to survey the damage but there was little to see. The dock was charred and roped off, so no one tried to climb on it. At least the fuel tanks at the end of the dock were intact.

After stepping back to the smaller dock, she sat on *Wanderlust* and looked out at her island. Suddenly she knew why she had the life jacket. There were ropes and clamps in the storage locker under the captain's chair. Inside she found just what she needed, and she strapped the life jacket to the front of *Wanderlust* like a figurehead. It had been her good luck charm and would be in the future. And would make a great conversation piece.

"It's good to see you back," a voice called out from on the sand. The voice belonged to Sam.

She owed him an explanation.

"It's good to be back," Dani said as she stepped off her boat and walked toward him. "I need to talk to you. I need to explain myself. I...I was trying to save my brother, which is why I didn't show up for work. I understand if you want to fire me."

Sam waved his hand to shush her. "You don't owe me an explanation for trying to save Cody. He's family.

But next time, and I hope there isn't a next time for your sake, trust the police to help you."

"Yes, I will, but I don't expect there to be a next time." She shifted back and forth from foot to foot, nervous about her next statement. "Do you need me tonight?" She knew there were always dirty dishes.

"We haven't had a lot of customers since the fire. People are keeping pretty close to home and there aren't a lot of tourists. Why don't you take the night off and rest. I'll need you tomorrow night."

Dani smiled and sighed in relief. She still had a job and with the condition of the dock, there wouldn't be as many fares for a while as in the past. "Thank you," she said and then watched Sam walk away. He waved at String who had just shown up with a commuter cup in hand. Without speaking, they stepped back on her tour boat. Whatever was in the cup they shared. It tasted like mango, and they enjoyed it as they watched the sun set.

It was good to have him around even if they were doing nothing.

Chapter 40

Like a second miracle, the first being his survival, Cody's doctor got him into a ninety-day treatment program at a Corpus Christi rehab facility. He'd gone through the worst of the withdrawals without help in the grimy motel and then later drifting at sea. But he needed more guidance to help him not fall back the way he used to live. He happily signed the paperwork and then called Dani giving her the details.

Her heart sang with joy. This was exactly what she hoped for. Maybe her little brother was really coming back to her again. The boy she played with as a kid. The boy who told Mom it was his fault Dani wasn't wearing her life jacket. Maybe he'd even be a partner in her business.

Dani had no way to go see him—if that was even allowed. She had no car and even though she could take the ferry to Corpus, she couldn't get to the rehab facility unless it was near the bus route. Her uncle had taught her to pilot a boat while she was still in grade school, but she had never learned to drive a car. She'd always said she had no money to buy one anyway, so what did it matter—until now.

But they both had cell service.

She talked to Cody on the phone daily. He called her when he wasn't in counselling sessions. And she waited. It seemed ninety days was like a million years. She wanted to see her baby brother and make sure he was okay.

Back at the mooring for *Wanderlust*, Dani looked in the distance. The tour boat that had been abandoned was anchored offshore. When the flames began, the big commercial tour company left the island. One had been burned and left behind. From where she stood, it didn't look damaged. Maybe she should look. She untied *Wanderlust* and pointed it in the direction of the tour boat that was sitting out in the water.

It didn't take long to reach the spot where the larger boat was anchored. She climbed aboard the other boat after tethering the two together and looked around. There was no one there, but if they showed up, she'd just say she was kicking the tires, or whatever you said when you were looking to buy a used boat.

The boat was much bigger than hers, but it was piloted in much the same way. She walked to the helm and started the motor. It sounded smoother than her own. It would carry more passengers and if the price were right, she and Cody could have it paid for quickly. Roaming around its interior she leaned over the edge. All she could see was some smoke damage to the outside of the boat. It would need to be repainted and that could happen here on the island if the paint shop could get to it. This could be a godsend.

She would contact the owner and see how much they wanted for it and then she'd talk to the bank. Her tour boat was almost paid for, and she'd been a good customer. She had a small downpayment in the business account she had opened. This could work out. She and her brother were alive and now they could work together—just like they used to play together when they were kids. The sea was once more looking out for her. Her life was improving every day.

Chapter 41

Sam was right. There weren't as many customers since the dock burned. Not as many dishes to wash and not as much for the restaurant staff to do. But there were always dirty dishes. Then she heard Paul. His booming voice was hard to miss.

"How are you doing, lady?" Paul said behind her as she rinsed the final dishes and wiped the countertops. Most customers weren't allowed in the back, but Paul was the exception. And he normally went wherever he wanted to go anyway.

"Hello, Paul. I'm doing fine. How are you? I don't think I've said how grateful we all are that the fuel tanks didn't explode the night of the fire."

"Well, that's what neighbors are for. And besides, I use that fuel like you do. More than you do! It would have been disastrous for all of us if it had blown."

"Yes, it would have," Dani said as she dried her hands. "Meg told me that one of the big tour boats was damaged in the fire. She said the fleet left the island and went back to Corpus. But one boat is still anchored in the water and Meg says it's for sale. Do you know anything about that?"

"Are you interested?"

"I might be depending on the price, amount of damage, and the bank. Cody will get out of rehab soon and I'd like to expand my business and provide him with a boat so he can give tours too. He needs a break and we both need the income."

"Yes, they talked to me before they left, and I have some information that you can have. I think the bank would be happy to help you get a second boat."

Sam walked from the front in time to overhear the conversation wiping his hands on his apron and the sweat from his brow. "I am not trying to overhear your conversation, but I've been thinking, and I have a business deal for you if you're interested, Dani. What do you say to a dinner cruise? We could combine our efforts—you have the boat—I provide the food. We could both make some money and make some customers happy. I expanded a few years ago with the deck and live music. Now we can go into partnership for dinner cruises around the island. On nice evenings, intimate groups for special occasions or just for dinner on vacation. I think we could both make some money whether you get the second boat or not. And make some customers happy. Word of mouth is always the best advertisement."

Dani was dumbfounded. She could actually expand her business whether she bought a second boat or not. And she could present this idea to the bank to show that she was working toward building her business, not just borrowing money for another boat. "That sounds wonderful, Sam. I think we should try to do it whether or not I buy a second boat. Of course, if I'm on tour, I won't be able to wash dishes."

"Well, Cody will need a job when he gets out. You two could share duties."

Paul stood behind Sam listening to the conversation, never one to be shy. "Well, you two are going to need a lot more shrimp!"

****

Dani carried her evening meal home to her upstairs apartment and grabbed a beer from her fridge. She took them to the deck of her apartment that looked over the top of Le Chez and out into the harbor of Sandhill Island. She sat down on the wooden deck and quickly realized her jeans rubbed the still sore abrasions she had gotten the night she was clinging to the buoy. She normally wore shorts, but she washed dishes in jeans. The jeans would be more comfortable if she wasn't sitting on the rough wooden deck. She needed to find a lawn chair—two in case she had company.

She leaned her head against the siding of the apartment and looked in the distance as she ate her dinner. Her life had changed in so many ways recently.

Tomorrow she would ride with Shayla to Corpus Christi to get her brother home. It sounded like Shayla had been visiting Cody a lot and maybe their relationship was blooming. And that made her think of String. There had not been music at the restaurant tonight, but she hoped to see him tomorrow night.

Chapter 42

The tiny, sun-bleached life jacket hung proudly like a figurehead on the front of *Wanderlust* as a reminder of what Dani and Cody had been through. Faded and worn as it was, it would never be removed. The new boat was being painted for Cody to pilot. Once they had it, he could name it and it would be his. Dani would always feel a part of *Wanderlust* and being trusted with the new tour boat would make Cody feel a part of the business. But for now, they shared the one boat.

Cody was doing well after his time in rehab and told his sister he had a purpose in life this time. She felt she had to give him a chance. She owed it to him. They owed each other a lot.

Dani saw more of Shayla all the time as she and Cody spent more time together. She was becoming more than a friend to her brother.

The first dinner cruise on *Wanderlust* hosted Paul and his wife, Becky. They would be able to have larger crowds when the new boat was ready. The cruise went smoothly with just Dani, the waiter, and two guests. To work more efficiently, they would need more practice. The idea was sound, but the logistics might take a little longer to work.

****

Sam invited the entire island to dine with them at Le Chez as a renewal of spirit dinner. String and Billie provided music and when they finished Billie joined Neil for dinner. They sat at the table with Paul and Becky and talked about the night of the fire. Neil described finding Dani clinging to the buoy in the harbor. He laughed when he told of Billie fighting off the shark with a paddle from his boat.

They pulled up a second table to join theirs when Martha, Sandy's mother, came in. Billie's best friend from childhood, Sandy, and her kids quickly followed. In the noise of the restaurant, you could still hear Billie's laugh as she hugged her friend. Sandy and her kids had driven in from Biloxi and everyone marveled at how much her kids had grown. "They'll eat you out of house and home," Sandy said about her kids who were now as tall as she was.

Jon Stanford and his new wife sat at a table with his mother, Meg. Jon's wife had been the nurse who helped Meg in the hospital in Corpus Christi after the hurricane a few years ago, and she and Meg had developed a wonderful relationship. Jon had given up waiting on the quaint ferry and bought a boat he could pilot himself to the island anytime he wanted to visit his mother. The plus was it was owned by the trust and could be used for other purposes. After all, they lived on the seashore.

"Oh, I'm so glad you could come," Meg said as they sat down and the men shook hands. Meg sat with Alex, who still had paint under his nails. His paintings were very popular on the mainland, and he always had commissions waiting. He was an islander these days, too, and wouldn't miss the dinner.

Betty and Guilda closed Auntie's Ice Cream Shack early so they could eat with Sienna. Her husband, Jake, was out on assignment mapping a section of the ocean where he hadn't been before and would be home in a few weeks.

The constables from law enforcement on the island had their own table and Special Agent Kent Murphy joined them. Most people didn't recognize The Cleaner without his disguise. But he told Riggs and Skaggs that Carlos had finally confessed to stealing *Wanderlust* and Joey was also behind bars on charges of arson, drug dealing, and conspiracy to commit murder.

It was obvious Murphy kept checking out Sandy who sat a few tables over and before the night was done, he had introduced himself.

The restaurant erupted into applause when Cody walked in accompanied by Shayla and a table was set up for them. Dani was still in the back but would finish soon and join the other diners.

Poppy was more comfortable eating on the dock with Blackie, so Sam saw that they were fed where they preferred.

****

Agent Kent Murphy, DEA, stood on the beach and looked out at the water. He looked like a tourist now and no one noticed him at all. He was the king of blending in. His compact stature didn't rise above the crowds and his haircut wasn't too short or too long to attract attention. Sometimes that was good, especially when undercover, and sometimes it was bad. He hadn't had a date in a long time. Mostly he worked.

No one knew he had actually grown up near the water and would like to retire there someday. Every time he traveled to a new place, he checked it out for potential retirement. That would be a long time, but it never hurt to look around. One thing about traveling for work was that you could see potential places to live. And he liked it here on Sandhill Island. This would be in his top ten places. The people were friendly, the beach was clean, and the food at one particular restaurant was great. As far as the women were concerned, he hadn't found one in particular, but he did meet a meteorologist with a couple of kids he liked. It was a long shot, but he played the long shot most of his life. Biloxi was on the water too and he found out that was where Sandy lived.

"Could I come by and visit with you next time I'm in Biloxi?" Murphy stood talking to Sandy as her kids played on the beach. She was heading home the next day.

"I'd love that." She smiled as she gave him her number and then called her kids.

"Time to go to Grandma's." Then squeezing his hand, "We'd love to see you. Call me."

Maybe he'd check out Biloxi sometime now that he'd made a friend there.

****

Back in Corpus Christi, Jimmy had finally run out of money and was tired of his waiting on a potential new boss. The junkies had finally quit showing up in the morning and went elsewhere. He took his backpack and walked back to the bus stop which took him to the ferry. He'd go home and talk to his family. Maybe his job would still be there. But still he planned to leave the island he'd grown up on, but not until he had the resources and somewhere to go. He could surely do better for himself than working for a drug dealer anyway.

The sea breeze blew his hair from his face as he crossed the strand of water that divided the island from the mainland and then walked back to his parents' home. He hoped he would be welcome.

****

Dani and Cody talked to the County Attorney from Corpus Christi and gave him all the information they had on Joey in exchange for no criminal charges being brought against them. They were just pawns in a bigger scheme. The men on the cigar boat were never found but Carlos was arrested for stealing Dani's boat. He too would testify against Joey for a lesser sentence.

Joey might not see the light of day for a while.

****

Dani finished her shift at Le Chez and wiped her hands on the towel that was then thrown into a laundry pile. She was making good money working for Sam, and the new sunset dinner cruises would add to her profits, eventually. So far, Cody was sleeping on Dani's couch, now that he was home from rehab, but she knew he wanted a place of his own soon.

"You still haven't seen my new place." Dani turned around quickly to find String standing behind her.

"I've been meaning to. Things have been a little crazy, but I'd love to." She smiled.

He held up a bag that said Le Chez on the side. "It just so happens I have dinner for two from Le Chez. Care to join me? It's a short walk." He nodded toward the other end of the island.

"Everything around here is a short walk," she giggled—and she wasn't one to giggle. Her life had been tough up until now, but she saw good days ahead. They walked out the back door and onto the sand.

Talking in the moonlight as String carried their dinner, they walked past the new dock. It still smelled like fresh-cut wood, even though it was treated to be in and around the water.

The Stanford Trust had the sand dredged out that had washed into the harbor. The sandbar had ultimately saved Cody's life, but the lack of it now made the harbor safe for deep boats. It was sad to see it go—no more wading out farther than normal. But piloting a boat around it would not be as hazardous.

The young shark would have to find food in the deeper and more dangerous waters. He too had to watch out for predators. But Scar continued to patrol the area of the dock for his favorite humans and the fish they fed him.

Dani waved in the distance at her brother and Shayla sitting on the dock. They spent a lot of time together these days. She was so proud of him and the progress he'd made. The new boat was due next week and she had a place for it to dock next to *Wanderlust*. They had yet to name it. But Shayla was painting a sign for the dock that said "Island Tours by Capts. Dani and Cody Brown." The siblings argued over whose name came first but flipped a coin.

String reached for Dani's hand as he transferred the sack with dinner to the other. They walked off into the moonlight comfortable as old friends. Dani knew her life had taken a big turn for the better. She was lucky to be alive and so was Cody. She had a new apartment and a new friend with String. Where the friendship would go, she wasn't sure, but it felt comfortable.

Dani pulled off her shoes and waded through the tide pool on the beach. Even in the dark she could see the waves tumbling over each other in unison foaming up on the sand. They left tiny crabs and fish behind in pools. The next high tide would carry them back out to the deeper water. In their tiny world, life would go on as it should without the giant ocean reclaiming it. This was the Sandhill Island that Dani loved. She kicked her toe up and watched the water fly from the end of it and sparkle in the moonlight.

The sea breeze gently blew her hair from her face reminding her of why the ocean was her home. She had no desire to live in Corpus Christi anymore. She could rent an apartment on land and have a business on the ocean—just like Uncle Ralph hoped for her.

Dani could get used to standing on firm soil and the rocking of waves when she was on the water. She had the best of both worlds.

She and Cody had the best of both worlds.

A word about the author...

Peggy Chambers lives in her hometown of Enid, Oklahoma with her husband. She is an award-winning multi-genre author who loves fantasy, suspense, and children's books. There is always another story worming its way around in her brain trying to come out. She once climbed Chichen Itza, went on safari in Zimbabwe (where she ate wart hog pizza for lunch), snorkeled off the coast of Montego Bay, Jamaica, swam with the dolphins in Mexico, and still loves to travel. When not writing she gardens and is a member of four writing clubs. She has two children and five grandchildren. There aren't enough hours in the day!